God Is A Tequila Worm

Tim Rousseau

RUNNING WILD

RUNNING WILD PRESS

Paperback ISBN: 978-1-960018-45-8
eBook ISBN: 978-1-960018-44-1

For John

Contents

The First Turn

i

I flew my plane, and would continue to fly now, if not for this interminable bout of green-filled skies through the window. It is impossible to tell from where it came, nor how long it would remain, though I had my suspicions that it had come from that green Vietnam jungle blended with all that fire, and smoke, and death—a swampy summer heat accompanied the green. The sky now looks similarly hazy, and the light dances across the smoke, and the smoke conceals its origin, and as the light becomes more and more powerful, and longer and longer, the sky changes, and the air below holds that same green tinge. Inside, there is no green—it can't penetrate the walls around me—but outside it is killing, indiscriminate, vengeful. We have for so long savaged everything around us; it is only natural and expected that it, in turn, would come to savage us with its green air and poisons. One would think that revenge would come with a shift to red, that our greed would be perfectly envisaged in the yellow air after a storm, our mourning in the deep blue skies of twilight—but this is not human revenge filled with anger and hatred. This green comes as the byproduct of our greed, imbued with the character of mourning, for this whole world mourns for us and our follies.

It has been said as far back as my family has spoken that we are of the kings. William, the one who landed at Pevensey, sired William the Second, who then sired Henry, and on and on for fourteen generations until the Roses had their war, and the line apparently died. But lesser relatives survived and bided their time as commoners until they left their home for the supposed New Eden another fourteen generations later. It was then, fourteen or so generations after the exile, that I came into the world, a shining descendant of our tree, in a small hospital not far from Boston three years after the conclusion of the second Great War. We came from royal blood before our exile and relocation to this royal-less land; my grandfather was of that sort, always invested in origins and possible histories and the futures they could precede, caught between the glory of our supposed royal ancestry and the absurdity of his involvement as an American in this war of centuries-old royal agreements and aggression. In his retirement, my grandfather dedicated the last years of his life to cultivating our tree to bolster the legends against the naysayers with me, King Peter the Bloodless, destined to bring our family back into the royal fold. Fearing an insurmountable ego, my parents moderated my grandfather's stories and saw me off into my own pointless war, flying my plane off into the putrid green skies.

But just as I am king only in myth, so does the world mourn only by our own fancy. In truth, we are the only ones who mourn against our backdrop of fear at our own undoing, the perfect antithesis of our false royal violet. Just as I am no king, there is no air left to breathe; it has all been consumed by the green, and our collective life is quickly coming to an end. It is the greatest irony that green has for so long been the symbol of spring, new life, youth, inexperience, for I can tell you with certainty that is not the case. But the green doesn't care about ironies; the green only cares about death.

🍾

Johanna woke with a start from the depths of a dream that had consumed her and left her feeling as though she did not exist— that she had been reduced to a disembodied observer peering from an anti-plane upon characters living out the narrative of her life in her stead. When her breath ceased rattling between her ribs, when the sleep paralysis wore off and allowed her to rise in jolting movements through her small, gray bedroom to the sitting room qua all-inclusive modular living space, when she finally arrived to the chair by the waist-to-ceiling quasi-corporate window, de-tinting as she approached, she poured herself a slug of tequila from the bottle on the table in the corner, sat in her chair, and gazed out onto the glassy surface of steel-city reflecting artificial neon under the endless smog above.

🍾

For my part, I am safe inside for the time being. The walls and windows protect me from it until it will become clever enough to penetrate deep enough to consume me. But the inside is decaying and falling apart as well; it can only hold off the green for so long before it, too, succumbs to the green reclamation of all back to death. The walls around me are old, and chips have formed in the paint at the corners. Pictures hang at unnatural angles; all are faces I can no longer recognize covered over by the mists of time. Splinters from the rough-hewn floor dig at my numbed, rubbered feet in colorful woven patterns of reds, and blues, and blacks, not yet consumed by the green. Under me, my chair falls into tatters as I sit and stare—perhaps my chair is the locus of the green's siege of this house and where my final, futile stand against it will be held. To all those previously lost in the precursor to this totalizing collapse: I will soon be joining you, despite my most thorough protestations. Guilt permeates through the pores of everything—the indictment of my own inaction as much as anyone's—and overcomes any merit I may have earned for myself, any merit I may have inherited through severed bloodlines, and so now I come unto death, a death not fit for royalty.

As I mourn, a woman comes into my room from the kitchen; the green is in her eyes as well as outside, and she is beautiful with blonde hair falling to her shoulders; sharp, angled features, despite their retreat under bags and mounds of wrinkled skin. She smiles at me—a brief comfort from my terror, recognizing nothing but the green in her eyes; I am convinced my time has finally arrived—but she says nothing. I can hardly move my head or eyes or mouth to face or even greet her entrance into my kingdom (ah! More indictment against my royal lineage!), and she remains in the doorway, looking onto me before she speaks.

"Are you hungry? I'm going to make lunch."

Her words pass over me as a flurry of vibrations jostling across my skin, beautiful noise tingling inside my ears, and a wake of love passing through me. The words themselves are garbled, but I manage to decode one of them: hungry. The word gives me the fear of an execution and the love of a pet name uttered to implore before amplifying itself into a screaming rage, tightening me rigid to retaliate or resist attack. Soon it soothes to a familiar word: hangar. My plane, stored a quarter-mile from the runway—but not mine. I shared it on rotation with others, but most often flew it. Under me, instead of a chair, oceans sloshed, and wind blew through the tree branches and leaves along the small mountains and hills, then skyscrapers and the dark channels between them, then more mountains, bigger, now. As I flew that twin-jet carrying my human cargo, my dials turned analogue, and the sea below me birthed forth aircraft carriers and battleships making way for the jungle ahead of me. Smoke quivered out of the trees, with flames below consuming all the vegetation in insatiable hunger, and mingled around the wings, the engines. There had been a jolt, hard and to the right; the flight engineer grabbed my left shoulder and dragged me from my seat until I started moving on my own. I drifted down toward the ocean sloshing below me, coughing from the smoke, watching the plane continue flying itself off toward the horizon.

Johanna took a shaking sip and tried to steady away the residual terror from her breath. In the dream, she had watched a revolving series of characters—of a variety of genders, ethnicities, ages— cycling through the responsibility of carrying her avatar forward in life, depositing it to await the next in the cycle, with the switching starting slow and speeding up as she quickly approached her death, powerless to enact agency over the avatar that supposed the only embodiment she had been allowed in the logic of the dream.

All of these thoughts of death and destruction have left me craving a drink, and I look over to the cabinet. In moments like these of terror and confusion, God seems not to intervene, leaving it up to us mortals to find a salve for our pain. And what glorious salvation a stiff drink can be! That is the reason a drink is the cliché of a difficult day, a ponderous afternoon, an evening mourning lost loved ones. The liquor provides such a gratifying exhale in solitude, camaraderie lifting into song—whether to mourn or celebrate, or narcotic sweetness to overwhelm the bitter trials. A small belt of whiskey, either sipped gradually and stirred around the tongue lost in ponderous thought, or thrown back in a moment of brazen desperation against a harrowing chill. The flowery nose of a sweet gin, mixed with sparkling water or syrupped wine at the tail end of a hot day, battling away the sensation of lost time. The saltwater specter of a seafaring rum, mixed with juice or taken by itself to imagine the lives one could have lived. The crystal bite of a smooth toss of vodka to take the edge off the winter. A rippling sip off a snifter of brandy warmed against the palm of the hand to then go on to warm the soul against the encroaching cold. A crisp glass of wine to revitalize the blood and animate the body against the paralysis of a long hibernation. Or the special occasion that calls for the turpitudinous tequila, mixed or alone, sipped over ice, or hot as the summer sun and taken for the Holy Communion with divine ecstasy and worldly madness, baring the truth of one's soul, and opening one's eyes to nothing but that truth, as distorting as it may become. But here I am, so parched, so in need of those numbing waters that one drop of tequila might kill me outright and send me tripping along to talk to the tequila worm at the bottom of my glass—show me the way home to my maker. I look —the liquor cabinet isn't where it was, either moved or having not existed in the first place—it's no longer possible for me to know.

The woman stands over me with a blanket, dropping it onto my lap and tucking it into the sides of the chair—an inscrutable gesture as heat waves rise through the air outside. Back at the doorway, the woman smiles at me once more and is gone, presumably back to where she came from, leaving me to myself in my chair.

🍾

Finishing her drink, she poured another and set it next to herself. The dream still remained the centerpoint of a falling orbit her mind continued to cling to even as she consciously tried to sling-shot herself from its influence. Instead, she concentrated on the physical sensations around her—the rough texture of her badly upholstered chair through thin pajamas and up her back; the sickly-sweet fire of the tequila bubbling in her nearly-empty stomach; the cool, sterile air passing gently in and out through her slackened mouth. In the dream, she had not even the agency to feel the fear the lack of control imprinted upon her. She could comprehend that she was terrified, that her lack of control over her avatar constituted a cosmic betrayal perpetrated by an unknown traitor, but could not experience that white-hot horror in her noumenal form. The room in which she sat contributed no comfort either—the view of the burning engine of cityscape, the shadowed sterility of her living quarters, the pulsating hum emanating from the building itself locked her in a static mundanity.

I

At the last appointment they'd gone to the previous day, the doctor told them that Peter was in the final stretches of the illness and had strongly encouraged Sanna to check him into a care facility that was equipped to handle dementia cases. As always, she'd nodded and thanked the doctor for his time and expertise before taking her husband home. Other than the dementia, his health was fine for his age —the doctor had said so every time they'd been in his office. Like every other appointment she'd taken Peter to, Sanna asked the doctor how much time he had left. And like every appointment before, the doctor always replied that it would depend on a variety of factors which they couldn't possibly know ahead of time. But Sanna was a retired nurse, for chrissakes. She was more than capable of taking care of Peter. This was so even considering that for the last several months before the appointment, he'd been completely nonverbal, and shortly after that, seemed uninterested in getting out of his chair without her prompting, guiding hands—it was almost nothing to care for him. Despite his lack of response, she still talked with him during his everyday tasks—bathing, feeding, using the bath-room. To her, it kept them connected despite the communication barrier that had formed between them.

Now, it was midday, and Sanna stood by the stove, occasionally stirring a pot of soup for lunch. Deep into this bitter New Hampshire winter and holed up in the drafty, old colonial they'd bought almost forty years ago, she'd noticed Peter shivering slightly in the living room and hoped hot soup would warm him. Snow had fallen overnight and lay glistening through the kitchen window on the ends of tree branches, the railings on the back porch, along the paths leading around their backyard. Frost bit at the corner of the windows, vignetting the whole scene in refracted sunlight. For a moment, she had considered taking Peter for a walk through the snow—there was a gentle trail that started at the top of the street they used to walk through together most days since Sanna had retired—but thought better of it. He was still capable of walking, albeit with an arm under his to help support him, and exercise would be a benefit to someone so otherwise sedentary, but the effort it would take to collect all his winter clothes, bundle him up against the cold outside (not to mention the fact that he already was cold, sitting in his chair by the heater), seemed to outweigh the benefits of a walk, even one she so desperately craved for herself as well.

From the other room, Sanna heard a noise—guttural and uncoordinated, like a shocked yelp through a broken megaphone. She left the soup to continue simmering with the spoon-handle leaned against the side of the pot and rushed to the living room to check on Peter. As she walked through the doorway, Peter let out another yelp that startled her into stillness. He hadn't fallen and didn't otherwise look in pain; his diaper was dry when she checked, and nothing else seemed to be wrong.

"How're you doing?" she said without expecting a reply. He continued staring ahead, not acknowledging her presence, but yelped again, this time raspier and with less force. She waited to see if he would keep it up, but after several minutes of silence, she patted him on the knee and stood. "Lunch is almost ready. I'm sure you're starving." With a smile, she left him again, pausing for a moment in the doorway to look back at him.

ii

After her third glass of tequila that night, the shadows in Johanna's apartment began to fade into a uniform, pre-dawn gray—completely unthreatening, bland, and serving as nothing more than a generic backdrop. In this state, she felt embodied again, bolstered against her dream, having banished the residual specters, and now something burned in her which she could not quite place. It was not the tequila. That always went down easy and comforted the dull ache resonating between her shoulders, gut, and jaw. That always released the tension that arrived as if a toxin floating on the wind, inhaled, and lodged into the vital processes of her body. This was something else.

I woke against a semi-rigid mattress, bent at an angle to suspend my torso upright so I could gaze into the room I was in—sterile-white and filled with glass, metal, and easily cleanable plastics. An over-laundered blanket lay across my legs exposed by a thin gown and covered equally laundered sheets under me. A plastic tube ran from a needle sticking out of the top of my hand into a plastic bag above my head, while another ran from a clip attached to my finger and split toward several machines all punctuating the still air with polyrhythmic beats faithful only to their own individual rhythms. The room was sealed in by plate-glass windows on one end of the room overlooking a landscape I could not see at this angle, and by a blinds-covered glass wall. Locked in between the sky-only view through the windows and the rigid plastic blinds on the other, I focused my attention to the far wall, wallpapered in a vinyl floral pattern and suspending a small tube television hanging on brackets. Too-thin armchairs sat below it for absent guests. As I became aware of my surroundings, I became aware of an aching in my arms and shoulders under a cast that ran up each arm and in front of and behind my neck like football pads.

The aching soon became worse, my mind grew sharper, and whatever medications were in my system continued to wear off. Inside my shoulders, I felt pieces of myself grating together. I struggled for perfect stillness, but still had to breathe, and so pain still radiated down my arms in a pulse following the rising and falling of my chest. No position I could find felt comfortable or reduced the pain, and every movement I made sent out earthquake-like shocks, rending the tectonic plates along my body. I breathed my way through the pain in as much stillness as I could muster before looking for some way to call a nurse. Beside my bed, a remote sat on a small table, tempting me to endure the inevitable pain of reaching for it with thoughts of the narcotic bliss that would soon arrive if I could reach it. My arms, of course, had been plastered rigid and suspended at chest level requiring me to twist my entire body at my hips to get close enough to the table. I was able to twist a few inches in either direction, rocking back and forth for momentum, but the suspension held me firmly in place.

Before I could rock myself to the remote, a blonde woman in a lab coat walked in from the door with a chart under her arm and piercing green eyes. I stopped rocking my body and tried to breathe through the pain that it had caused as I stared at her face, transfixed by her eyes and desperate to remember where I knew her from.

"Please don't rock in the bed, if you can help it," she said, pulling up a chair and sitting next to my bed.

"I was trying to reach the remote." She followed my gaze to the bed-side table and took it in her hands, pressing one of the buttons on its face. With a buzz, the top of my bed moved up slightly, and I winced. She smiled and put the remote back on the table.

"We're going to avoid narcotic pain meds if we can, but I'll send a nurse in with some ibuprofen on my way out. Looks like it's just a broken collarbone—granted a hell of a break, or breaks, rather—but a collarbone break just the same."

"What happened?"

"Believe it or not, an airplane crash." The woman leaned back in her chair and flipped through the chart in her hand, drumming on the back of the clipboard all the while. "The Coast Guard found you floating in the water; apparently, you were pretty quick to get out of the plane." Something felt wrong about the woman's report—her demeanor, that I knew her from somewhere, that it wasn't a plane crash I was in, but some other accident. Something felt misplaced. "Remarkably, there's no internal bleeding or anything worse than a couple breaks around your shoulders. We're going to keep you here for a while to make sure nothing pops up, but you should make a full recovery."

"Do I know you from somewhere?" I said. She cocked her head at me with a quick smirk.

A gentle twitch in one knee urged her to rise from her chair. A flutter in her chest. A quiet voice somewhere secret whispering words she could not make out.

"Not that I'm aware of. I don't recognize you at least." In a moment, she had a flashlight in her hand, shining in my eyes with flashes of light. As I recovered from the sudden dazzling, she returned the light to the breast pocket of her coat. "It's likely you have at least an exceedingly mild concussion; you may be a little disoriented or dizzy for a while. If it gets really bad, let someone know, but you should be fine." She stood from her chair and returned it to the wall before turning back to me with another smirk. "If you need anything, give a shout."

"I don't feel disoriented."

"That's good." She waited for me to register her joke. "I was kidding, by the way. Please don't shout. A nurse will be by in a minute to give you some pain meds."

She left me alone again in the room and closed the door behind her; I was still convinced I knew her from somewhere, still convinced that something about this hospital room, this bed, my presence here was wrong, altered somehow.

She rose and followed the voice, the fluttering in her chest increasing in intensity as she grew closer to her goal, arriving at

16

a box in her closet, emptying onto her bed, grasping the delicate sides of an old handheld computational device issued by her employer and forgotten in the most recent upgrade. As if in reverie, she went to work clearing away the old programs cluttering the disk, sweeping away the digital-ash, and opening the internal architecture to reform this cold, corporate structure into something new. When the space had been cleared, when the drive had been reduced to cold void, Johanna began to build. In a flurry, as if blown in by a strong gale, code entered the void and crafted a new world filled with light and land, vegetation, animals. She had created a paradise away from the brutal grind of her daily life, amidst it all, but hidden deep within it, out of reach of any but herself.

II

By the time she returned to the kitchen, the soup was boiling, and the bubbles collected on the surface, threatening to spill over the top. With a quick hand, she turned the stove off and searched for the spoon—the roiling liquid had toppled the handle over into itself. Fast enough to not scald her fingers, she plucked the spoon out of the calmed broth and threw it into the sink. From a container next to the stove, she took another cooking spoon and returned to stirring the pot, sedate, as if nothing had happened. From the refrigerator she took a package of chicken she'd previously cubed and dumped it into the pot to join the broth, spices, and vegetables already cooking. Continuing to stir, she used the spoon to break the chicken apart from itself, freeing each piece to cook independently in the hot, swirling liquid. Only at this point did she turn the stove back on to continue cooking.

She thought that anyone who saw her here making lunch while taking care of Peter would be instantly convinced that she had the whole situation under control. The doctor's concern had made sense to her, but all he'd seen was the two of them visiting the office, and all he knew was his experience with the average family. He hadn't seen her at work, in her home environment, caring for her husband through sickness and health. Had he, she thought, he would have made a very different recommendation. Even when she started her own practice, years ago, she was more or less independent of the physicians that so frequently tried to give her unsolicited advice. That was the worst part of her time on the nursing staff at Anderson: the revolving door of physicians giving orders and exuding their arrogance. Her move to private practice improved the situation somewhat; Dr. Harper was easier to handle than an entire roster of physicians, but he still had moments she couldn't stand. As soon as she was able, she left with glee to start her own practice. Over her career, she'd dealt with far worse cases than Peter's current case: unruly patients, rude comments, cascading symptoms. Compared to her most troublesome patients, Peter may as well have been in perfect health. What's more, she didn't have the same depth of feeling for those patients as she did for her husband. She wasn't even completely sure why she allowed herself to continue justifying her decision in her head. She would care for Peter, end of story, come what may.

With the new spoon, she took some of the broth to her lips, sucked in just enough to taste it, and added more spices as she saw fit. According to the clock, the time was ten after twelve; the soup would be ready to serve in only a few more minutes and, with luck, cool enough to feed Peter by half-past. Stepping away from the stove for a minute, she took two bowls out of the cupboard and set them on the counter next to each other with a soft clink.

iii

The memory drains from my face and rushes in and out, with the doctor running in and out of my room, back and forth like a VCR stuck on a ripped tape. On each repetition, her eyes flash at me in their bright green greeting, piercing and flowing into the room. One step in, one step out, over and over until she has taken her forty steps toward me, and her forty steps back, and the time has been passed.

🍾

Johanna had no answer, now that she had fallen out of trance, why she would build something of this sort.

🍾

Her hospital badge jangles on the end of a clip on her lab coat all the while—Doctor Bertrand Munro. Had she stolen these credentials? Munro certainly wasn't this doctor's name; the woman I knew had a different name, more comforting and that flicked off the tip of the teeth when you spoke it. The woman I knew lived in Illinois; was I back in Belleville somehow? Back on base? The woman freezes in the doorway with her chart, mouth open to chastise me for rocking in the bed, and the dates begin to slip from my mind—my age is a mystery, the hospital room doesn't look like the ones near the base, I am now trapped in bed while this woman I don't know looks in on me. I wanted to get out, to leap from the window by my bed and be caught by the angels, transported safely to the ground, where they would clue me into the mystery of my presence here. Was this the concussion the woman spoke of?

All she could point to was the work of a phantom pulling her from her stupor and depositing her here, on her bed, as the sun tried to burn through the smog and artifice outside, encoding creation into the hollowed out shell of an obsolete device she had once been a slave to. But the act itself had made her happy.

The memory was false; I suddenly remembered. I was in a chair in a waiting room—not on base—one of the too-small armchairs that kept me from moving comfortably while sitting, with a small tube-TV suspended over my head and wires hanging down from it, snaking into the wall. The woman with the chart called me in from the waiting room and, through the doors to the hospital, antiseptic washed into me. She took me through the wards—so many sick around, suffering through their ailments. I wished them well, wished them better, wished them passage through the trials they faced. They spread through the wards in great crowds, wailing, and moaning, and dying, and I walked through helpless, giving up my wishes to something greater to heal these people. I hung my head as I followed this woman with the chart to a room.

Inside, the room was filled with glass, and metal, and easily cleanable plastic. A bed lay with its head against the side wall, and a scraggly, bearded man lay under a blanket as his sun-beaten, scarred-up skin sank into the sheets under him. Blood spots littered the skin on his face, and hands, and the edges of his fingernails, and the whites of his eyes had become tinged with yellow. Tubes ran from his arm and led to popping and humming machines, pulsing in their rhythms. The man in bed looked up and smiled when he saw me. Old Charlie Cannon lay in the bed, laughing at my sudden appearance to his bedside.

"Hastings, you son-of-a-bitch. What the hell're ya doin' here?"

"The guys at the VFW said you'd had a heart attack, or something," I said and looked at the woman next to me for confirmation. She didn't reply, or move, instead standing like stone to my right, listening to the two of us speak.

"Those poor bastards wanna do nothing but mourn; for me, for their timid, little lives," he said, sitting up in his bed and leaning on his IV'd arm. "You and I, we hunger for something more than that, and so we drink to it, and we find our mercy in it."

"What happened, then? Are you doing ok?" I dragged a chair from the wall to his bedside, and he eased back down onto his pillows. The woman remained in the doorway, still as stone and not acknowledging our conversation.

"Well, there ain't nothing wrong with my heart, I'll tell you that. It's as pure and healthy as can be, as far as I can tell. The doc told me I passed out, and they want to figure out why. But I'm sure it's fine; they really need to calm their tits." I sit nodding with nothing to say in reply to Charlie, typical in our conversations. He laughs again. "Those fuckers are probably all just sitting down there gossiping like old ladies about me and my hospital stay. Let me tell you, they need to get hobbies, every one of 'em. Do me a favor; go have a drink tonight—I'm paying—give a toast to the tequila worm in my honor, and if you hear anyone talking shit, go give 'em a good wallop for me, yeah?"

She found herself smiling, and tears burst forth as she recognized how long it had been since she had felt anything other than a strangling numbness. As the sun continued to rise, she stared on in awe as long as she could before her alarm went off, ushering in another wave of fear. This one was different from the one she awoke to hours prior. Where the former was the dread of a creeping nihilism, this fear was born of an almost parental love. Quickly, she hid her creation away and prepared for her commute.

Behind me the woman had taken a couple steps forward, drawing my attention away from Charlie. Still rigid, she opened her mouth to speak, and out came the sound of a telephone ringing.

III

As she set the bowls down on the counter next to the stove, the phone on the wall next to the refrigerator began to ring in its irritating chime. Sanna gave the pot of soup a quick glance and a quicker stir before pulling the phone off the receiver.

"Hello?" she said into the mouthpiece as she returned to the stove to keep an eye on the soup.

"Hi, Mom, how are you?"

"Lucy, is that you?" Sanna took the spoon handle in her hand again, testing the softness of a piece of potato.

"Yes, it is. How are you?"

"Oh! Wonderful to hear from you. How are you and Dylan? Is Maddie enjoying her winter break?"

"Everyone's fine here; same as always. Maddie starts school again next week. What about you and Dad?" Sanna turned to lean on the counter next to the stove, holding the phone in one hand and the edge of the stove in the other as the spoon slid around the inside of the pot, coming to a stop at an odd angle a few inches clockwise from where she set it down.

"Oh, you know. We're both fine. Your father's in the living room, and I'm making the two of us lunch. A nice vegetable soup. I got the recipe online; there's this website I found. I can't quite remember the name off-hand, but I have it bookmarked—"

"That sounds lovely, Mom."

"It smells wonderful. This is my first time making it, and I'm excited to try it."

"Doctor Munro called me this morning. He said Dad had an appointment yesterday? How's he doing?"

"Oh, the doctor is fine. He seemed a little tired—"

"Mom, not the doctor. How's Dad? How'd the appointment go?" Sanna chewed her lip for a moment and batted her fingers against the glass stovetop.

"You know, he's alright. Did the doctor tell you? Your father is as close to perfect health as he could hope to be for his age. Actually, the doctor is getting up there in age, too. Did he mention anything to you about his own health? Like I said, he seemed really tired when we were there."

"That's not... No. Mom, did Munro talk to you about checking Dad in somewhere?"

"Of course not. Your father's in perfect health." Sanna pushed off the counter and glanced through the doorway into the other room as she waved her freed hand to punctuate Peter's health. Lucy kept quiet on the other line, leaving a light static between them along with a faint whirring, before taking a soft breath.

"Munro told me over the phone he thinks Dad would be well served in some kind of care facility." Sanna laughed out loud, overselling her ridicule.

"Nonsense. What, do you think your father is some invalid bumbling around this house alone? He has me to take care of him."

"What I'm saying is he could have full-time nursing care—"

"He has full-time nursing care. I was an NP wasn't I? Or did I dream the last fifty years of my life?"

"You know that's not what I mean. It can't be easy on you; you're almost the same age as him." Sanna returned to the stove and stirred a bit of foam that had begun to form on the surface of the soup back in with the rest. Her hand moved in calm, slow circles as it mixed.

"I appreciate your concern. I really do. But I can promise you, we have everything under control here. There's no need to worry."

iv

A woman, a different woman, brunette and eyes not of green but of piercing, icy blue, her hair locked to her scalp in bundles, her clothes tight and modern, sits on a low stone wall by a long parking lot filled with cars that wraps around an institutional, brick building. An ambulance races from the street into a covered overhang on the far side of the building, screeching sirens echoing off the pavement and brick until the whole scene comes to a silent stop. The woman scans the edge of the parking lot, stopping on each of the doors leading out of the building and straining against the distance to make out the identities of the people who come and go. The blonde woman—the doctor—her hair now tied back into a ponytail, walks out the door third farthest from the edge of the building. The woman on the wall launches herself off to intercept.

"Doctor Hastings!" she says. Doctor Hastings stops and turns, waiting for the woman to catch up, jingling her car keys in her hand. "I was worried I was going to miss you."

"Can I help you with something?" Doctor Hastings says.

27

"Not me, no. But I think I can help with your patients. Some of them, maybe. I hope."

"Is that so?" The woman flicks her fingers against her leg and paces, keeping in constant motion as she talks. Doctor Hastings glances around her and grips her keys between her fingers, preparing for an attack.

"My name is Lucy. I'm a physics researcher, and I received some burns—radiation burns— from an experiment I was doing. The experiment failed, and I went to the hospital to be treated. But by the time I got here, the burns had healed. The intake nurse turned me away, and I puzzled about it. But then I realized: the experiment had been a success."

"I'm glad you got better." Doctor Hastings takes a step around the woman but the woman, in her pacing, cuts her off.

"So am I. But you don't understand; the experiment was trying to produce a substance, one I think could be used to treat your patients. A panacea of sorts."

"That's wonderful," Doctor Hastings says. She tries to step around the other woman again, but is again cut off. "If you'll excuse me, I have somewhere to be. But I look forward to reading about your discovery when the research is published."

"Wait, please. Listen to me. The research won't be published; it's not through a legitimate lab. I was fired, but I *had* to continue my research." Lucy turns, wildly speaking. Doctor Hastings rolls her eyes and slips past her, walking faster now to her car. "Wait, you have to listen to me. I'm telling you—this is a revolution, but I need to test it and make sure I'm right." Doctor Hastings turns back to the woman.

"I just got off a twelve-hour shift, I'm tired, and I have somewhere to be before I finally get to go home and have a drink. So I'm going to leave now."

"You don't understand—"

"No, I don't. But, like I said, I look forward to reading your research when it's published." Lucy launches herself at Doctor Hastings and grips her shoulders.

"You're not going to slip away from me! This is too important. I think I've found an infinite source of creative energy, and if I'm right, you can heal so many people with it." Doctor Hastings swings at the woman with her keyed fist, barely missing her chin. Lucy leaps back, letting go of Doctor Hastings, allowing her to escape into her car, start the ignition, and pull out of her parking space. She runs a few steps after the car as it pulls onto the main road and disappears into traffic. "You're a doctor!" Lucy yells after the car. "There are sick people who need you!"

In the weeks that followed, Johanna's routine evolved into fidgeting her way through repetitive work days and mind-numbing commutes to come home and watch in awe as her creation developed, now on its own, in the box in her hands. Somehow, she had created something which she had never experienced before—the gentle sloshing of oceans against crumbling sand, the dull wind rustling through leaf and fur and blade of grass, the gentle touch of sunbeams.

IV

S anna waited on the line for an answer from Lucy. That static came and went as if rolling up and down the mountains that surrounded the house. Sanna peered through the doorway to check on an unmoved Peter and then returned to the stove.

"Ok, fine," Lucy said. "Mom, Ed and I are driving up."

"Right now?"

"Right now. We left early this morning."

"That's such a long drive." Sanna idly stirred the soup in the same, slow circles, her voice following the cadence of the spoon.

"It's fine, we wanted to see you, to talk in person."

"We'd be happy to have you. When do you think you'll be here? I'm not sure I can hold lunch for you, but I can set some aside."

"We're about an hour out. Don't worry about lunch, we already ate."

"Well, I'm looking forward to seeing you. You said Ed's with you, too?"

"He's driving." Sanna smiled and glanced up through the window.

"Well make sure he drives safely. The roads are all icy around us."

"We will. See you in an hour or so."

Sanna hung the phone back up on the receiver, holding the spoon still in her other hand. After a moment, she noticed it dripping on the floor and rushed back to the pot to set it back in, turning off the stove again. Taking a sheet of paper towel from the roll above the sink, she wiped the floor before starting to serve the soup she'd just finished into the bowls on the counter.

V

From her office cubicle—black plastic separating her
from a sea of white plastic desks, mounted tablet
screens, the ever present, sickly glow from windows no
one was close enough to see through from their desks—she
received a notification from the hundredth floor. They were
summoning her, the big bosses at the top of the The Company
ladder.

Through the kitchen window, two children play in the yard, a
young girl and her younger brother. They run over rocky soil,
chasing one another, until they stop by a swing-set purchased
from the hardware store and built upon the only cleared and
flat ground among the trees. Their youthful joy springs forth
with their leaps and bounds from the ground. The young boy
sits in one of the swings and calls his sister to push him. Up and
down he goes, too young to thrust himself into the arc, but
young enough to holler with glee as he flies through the air. At

the far peak of his swinging, a glint comes over the young girl's eyes. As the young boy returns, the girl digs her feet into the ground and takes hold of the chains as the boy swings away back toward the peak. The swing holds, and the boy is flung from his seat knee-first into the rocky soil, sliding several inches before falling on his face, in tears.

The girl watches her brother writhing on the ground, still holding the chains, unsure what to do, navigating whether this was the result she sought. After a moment, she sits in the swing she just evicted her brother from and rocks on her toes, observing her brother like a science experiment. Her brother's wailing calls their mother, the blonde woman with the piercing green eyes, and dirt-covered hands, and dirt-covered clothes. The mother appears from the side of the house, running to aid her injured son.

"Lucy!" the mother shouts. "Why would you do that to your brother?" The girl looks up, broken from her scientific reverie over her brother, and begins to cry, now realizing punishment is imminent. The mother crouches by her son, pulling him onto her lap, their hair nearly matching one another. Both knees ooze blood mixed with dirt, and the skin on his palms are ragged, but not quite bleeding. "Are you ok, Edmund?" The boy nods and passes his gaze between his mother and his sister, looking for some explanation for this wanton cruelty. "Apologize to your brother, right now. We don't push people." With her mother's indictment, a new burst of tears wells up in her eyes, and she shakes her head, terrified to admit her guilt. With one last wail, the young girl leaps from her seat and tears across the yard, in through the kitchen door, and up the stairs to her bedroom with the slam of a door.

After a moment of breathing and processing, staring unblinking at the screen, she rose and shuffled through the cubicles to the elevator. As she passed coworkers, they glanced up briefly at her and returned to their work with a confused, but ultimately uninterested expression. People quit and were fired midday often enough, processed and announced impersonally to the employee in question, and Johanna's demeanor closely resembled those of former employees except for one thing. Instead of glowering around as she processed to the door, she maintained rigid eye contact with it, startling when it opened merely upon her proximity.

🍾

The blonde woman hoists her son onto her hip and carries him —face still stained with tears, but no longer screaming— through the yard and into the kitchen. By the time they reach the kitchen, the young boy's tears have stopped, and he is only sucking in air in ragged breaths.

"Is he ok?" I say.

"Just a couple scrapes. He'll be fine."

"Sh-she pushed m-me, Daddy," the young boy says, stuttering through his uneven breaths.

"One of us needs to talk to Lucy," the woman says. "She didn't apologize."

"I can talk to her."

🍾

"Thank you, Johanna," a digital voice said over a loudspeaker once the doors closed. "We appreciate your speedy response to our summoning." The elevator slowly accelerated up to full speed as Johanna was left in the slightly whirring silence. After a

*couple minutes, her stomach lurched as the elevator slowed to a
stop. "You have now arrived at floor one hundred. Please wait in
the lobby and someone will come when they are ready to see
you." The doors shut behind her, and she could hear the elevator
receding back down its shaft as she sat in a rigid, black chair on
the far wall.*

Leaving the mother to treat her child's wounds, I follow Lucy's
path through the living room and up the stairs to her shut-up
bedroom. Through the door, she continues to cry in sobs and
bursts. I knock, and her response is to weep harder, so I return
down the stairs; she is clearly horrified at what she'd done so
scientifically and emotionlessly. She only wanted to know what
it would be like to cause pain; it wasn't that she enjoyed it. She
had tested it, rejected it, and was sure to apologize later, after
she satisfied her self-imposed, penitent isolation. Shut in by her
door and surrounded by her corrugated metal walls, her peni-
tentiary is not her bedroom, but a laboratory filled with piping,
and heat, and machines pumping and grinding in the small,
reverberant space. Lucy is an adult, long, brown hair hanging
down her back with piercing blue eyes searching along the trail
of piping, checking for any potential problems that may arise.
Her penitence has not ended, still searching for a cure for pain
and suffering.

With her, a man her age fumbles with a connection, trying
to screw two pieces of piping together and having trouble
aligning the threads. The man is not her brother; his features
are much darker, and his hands are much more confident.
Content with her survey, she turns to him.

"We ready to start?"

"Just have to catch these threads," he says. The piping

catches, and he spins them together until they're tight. "Got it." Sitting up, he joins Lucy by a control panel and watches her initiate the system with a series of button-presses. At the last one, an unseen engine whirrs up and reverberates into a deafening rumble. The room shakes, and the machinery rattles as Lucy watches dials move on the control panel. The machine hits a peak, catching the resonant frequency of the room, nearly pulling the walls down. Lucy leaps across the unsteady floor and turns a valve that had started to shake loose, resealing the machine. The man braces against the wall to keep from falling as the rumbling feeds back onto itself, and the shaking in the room gets worse and worse. Lucy tightens the valve again, sealing a canister away from the rest of the machine. Piping falls across her arm—searing hot—leaving angry red lines across her forearms and shoulder. With a shudder, she pushes the piping off her as the machine finishes its cycling and shuts off. The isolated canister continues to shake as if something living is inside, as if it is in the process of birthing something.

"Did it work?" the man says, letting go of the wall and taking a step toward Lucy. Lucy, breathless, says nothing and takes a step closer to the canister to inspect it. The rattling slows and the canister is motionless in its place.

"Holy shit, I think it did."

The canister explodes, sending Lucy flying back toward the man against the wall, nearly missing contact with his body as she collides with the wall. She falls to the ground, flayed by shrapnel and roasted by the energy contained within the canister. The man takes brief refuge behind the control panel, escaping the brunt of the explosion, but the force of it, and the heat expelled, sets the machine on fire, melting components and filling the room with a thick smoke. He pulls Lucy, unconscious, from the floor and carries her out of the room—a storage unit among many along the hall outside. Alarms blare as emergency vehicles arrive outside, ready to put out the fire, unaware of the radioactivity seeping into the air. The man runs for the door, unwilling to wait for an ambulance for Lucy, instead carrying her through the crowds of people gathered to watch the firefighters work, on their way to the hospital.

A middle-aged man, peppy in step, wearing a tight black suit appeared from down the hall. His lilting voice covered for his body's betrayal in drooping skin, reddened eyes, and an overall gray appearance. "They're ready for you now. Please follow me." Johanna stood and felt the room spin around her for a moment, halting her. The man turned and smiled. "First-timers sometimes feel dizzy this high up. It will pass. Please follow me." All of this with the same uncannily chipper tone. Recovering herself, Johanna followed the man down the hall to an enormous conference room at the far end of the building, this one ensconced not in tinted glass, but mirror-like aluminum marked with swooping, anodized designs along its length. The man knocked on a translucent glass door around an obtuse corner and ushered her inside before leaving her alone in the room with fifteen other people, all adorned in the same, tight-fitting formal suits cut in subtly different, though uniformly elegant ways, sitting along the outside edge of a semi-circle table with a small rectangular protrusion making it appear like the profile of a mushroom. This was The Board. Immediately, her discomfort spiked, and she drifted towards a chair that had been left for her at the foot of the rectangle and sank into it, feeling somehow lower to the ground than the fifteen others positioned around her.

Was Lucy the cause of this explosion? It was the man who'd stolen the equipment they blew up in the storage unit under Lucy's direction; he was her partner, and the one with access to the supplies they needed. She'd directed him, at his place of work, to stay late, and so he did, waiting in his office for the time when he was confident the rest of the staff had left. A woman had come to his door, his boss, knocking and leaning in through the open doorway.

"I'm headed out for the night," she said. "Do you need anything before I go?"

"No, I'm fine," he said. "I'm gonna stay a little late and finish up some paperwork. Have a good night."

"You too." The woman ducked out of the doorway for a moment, and then back in. "And Dylan, don't stay too late, ok?"

"Ok."

The woman disappeared, and her footsteps echoed down the hall, growing fainter with each step. Dylan's breath caught; it was time. Standing at his desk and taking one last, deep breath, he turned off his office light and walked down the hall to the storage room. The lights in the hall flipped on as he passed their motion sensors, causing a cascade of light to follow him as he walked. This was his moment to choose, and he chose to be with Lucy, his partner, come what may. The work she was doing was too important—an end to pain and suffering, an end to disease, a final refusal of death. There were risks involved, and they both knew this ahead of time and accepted it gladly. The cost of their own pain and suffering was a bargain compared to the abolishing of all human suffering henceforth. To Dylan, they were morally obligated to do everything in their power to run this experiment and to succeed.

But the canister explodes and throws Lucy against the wall. Shrapnel nicks Dylan's arms, cutting holes in his shirt, before he is able to fully take cover behind the control panel. Lucy crumples next to him as fires rage across the room. He leaps into action, hauls her over his shoulder, and runs from the ruins of their attempt. Each step echoes against the metal floors, and metal walls, and metal ceiling, all corrugated. Even the stairs are steel, rattling the whole way down to the street. Only from the outside can onlookers see that the building is made from concrete blocks held together by the interior steel lattice-work. Other onlookers gather as firefighters rush into the building with hoses, smoke pours up from the building, and the heat from the explosion pushes the flames to eat across the metal, setting the contents of other units ablaze.

A woman at the center of the semi-circle began: "It has come to our attention that you have been using company property to develop competing properties during company time," she said. "This is obviously a problem as it directly contradicts your employment contract."

"It wasn't on company time."

Passing through the line of emergency vehicles, Dylan continues to run, carrying Lucy's unconscious body in his arms, blood dripping onto his shirt from her wounds, sores forming along the lines of burns and irritated skin. Pedestrians he passes stare on in fright, exposed fully to the horrors normally contained in ambulances. With gasps of shock, they retreat out of the way, neither wanting to block Dylan's path nor being available to him for assistance, leaving Lucy's treatment entirely to the hospital. Her skin peels and falls away as the violence of Dylan's footfalls shake her body; blood congeals without scabbing, as if cooking into a smooth pudding. She gasps and chokes on dead cells and fluids collecting in her lungs, and Dylan picks up the pace, desperate to get her the emergency treatment she needs before she succumbs to her injuries.

At the hospital—Dylan is gone, leaving just the woman and the doctor—Lucy's wounds have healed, her sores have retreated back into her body, and the pallor that had previously covered her face has started to deepen and saturate in hue. Lucy lies in a hospital bed, conscious now, as Doctor Hastings hovers over her, inspecting the burns and shrapnel wounds.

"When did you say this explosion happened?" the doctor says.

"Not long ago, I don't remember when. I'm still a little disoriented."

"Not long, as in earlier today?"

"I think so."

Doctor Hastings' face puckers into a scowl as she continues inspecting Lucy's wounds. Moving from one to another, she shakes her head.

"Well, if ever you were looking for a sign that someone's watching after you, here it is." Doctor Hastings pulls her gloves off and throws them into the biohazard trash can on the floor. Lucy sits up on the bed, wincing against the residue of pain.

"What do you mean?"

"If I didn't know about the explosion, I wouldn't have believed you were injured today. Everything here looks like it's been healing for weeks now."

"Really?"

"I don't understand how it's possible. But there isn't much for me to do. Your body seems to be healing itself, and quickly." Lucy yelps, startling Doctor Hastings, who leaps from the seat she's just taken, and rushes to her patient. "Are you ok?" Lucy leaps out of bed.

"It worked!"

"Please, take it easy. Get back in bed."

"You don't understand, the experiment worked! I'm healing!" Doctor Hastings pushes Lucy back into her bed, trying to keep her as still as possible while checking the IV placement in her arm. "This is groundbreaking. I have to tell Dylan."

"You need to take it easy. We have no idea why you're healing this fast. Until we do, we need to keep you here in case this is a false flag and your symptoms come back or get worse." Lucy rolls her eyes.

"I'm taking up a bed from someone who's actually sick. I'm telling you, the experiment worked and I'm healed!" Doctor Hastings sighs and sits back in her chair, searching for reasons to convince Lucy to stay under observation. She stands again and takes a venipuncture kit from a cabinet.

"Let me just take some blood and have the lab process it, look for anomalies. If everything comes back normal, I'll discharge you. Until then, you stay here, you stay in bed. Agreed?"

"Fine." Doctor Hastings opens the kit and taps a vein in Lucy's arm, collecting a couple vials and covering the needle with gauze before pulling it out. She tapes a bandage over the withdrawal site and disposes of the kit in the sharps bin.

As Doctor Hastings leaves, Dylan isn't there; he's back home, or at the lab, or dead, or completely safe, having never participated in this scheme with her. But I was there, why? Dylan was back at home waiting for his wife to visit her mother and return, supporting from afar. I was down the hall, lying in my own hospital bed, waiting for my own old bones to heal from the injury I'd sustained. A plane crash, that's what the doctor had said; how was I in a plane crash? It'd been so long since I'd flown, I'd have been a passenger. I must've been a passenger.

The woman glanced over to the man sitting several seats down who pulled up the specific language on a tablet. "Employees are forbidden from any use, here conceived or otherwise conceivable, of company property with the purpose of developing program-ming architecture not in line with issued company technology or as instructed by a supervisor," he read. "Development of programming architecture includes, but is not limited to, a range of activities from the development of products intended to compete with company products or services to the alteration of technological architecture owned by the company for any reason."

"It wasn't on company time," Johanna repeated, holding her hands to her knees to keep them from shaking.

And so the plane jostles in the swirling turbulence containing and buffeting the cabin. We had taken off amid rain, trying to beat the storm into the air, and the pellets of water streaked across the windows. The passengers in my aisle grip their armrests and gasp at every drop and movement, holding the plane in the air by the sheer force of their fear of falling out of the sky—all those of little faith, sinking as they were into the bay below us. I lean back in my seat and close my eyes again to suffer through the chop as close to embodying an unconscious rag doll as possible. We had taken off just a few minutes ago but had made it past the initial dangers of takeoff. The plane thrusts its way through the clouds with fire at its back, continuing to gain altitude and ascend above the angry clouds and eddies of air.

A hush overcomes the cabin as the lights flicker, and the entire craft lurches at the mercy of the wind and rain around us. The engines die, and we drop, gliding down toward the bay below us in a tumultuous fall punctuated by the continued strobing of cabin lights, the battering of overhead baggage against the walls and floors and passengers, and the subsequent uproar of the passengers insistent against their participation in this plane crash. The craft is battered by the wind and turbulence as it falls in uneven increments, at one moment floating on a light updraft, the next again in free fall, the next shoved down to the earth by the force of wind shear. A flight attendant comes on over the radio.

"Attention, passengers, buckle in and brace for impact. I repeat: brace yourselves for impact."

The passenger to my left curls over into his own lap and screams prayers through his desperate gnashing of teeth and tears in hope of salvation from our current torment. The airframe groans and wails in its own desperate prayer for peace over the din of the other passengers as the weight of a kingdom bears it down into the sea. My body is locked rigid into my seat, not yet sure enough of the situation to begin fearing for my life, but aware enough that something was amiss that needed to be prepared for. The praying passenger to my left grabs my arm and pulls me down to my knees with him before continuing his prayers. I listen in, unable to form my own words as the waves of terror wash over me and drown the remaining peace in the empty parts of my body.

"Our Father, who art in Heaven, hallowed be thy name. Thy Kingdom come. Thy Will be done. On Earth as it is in Heaven. Give us this day our daily bread and forgive us our trespasses as we forgive those who trespass against us. And lead us not into temptation but deliver us from evil. Amen." Then a Hail Mary, Glory Be, rinse, repeat.

What are you hoping to be saved from? I consider asking the man to my left. *Embrace these last chaotic moments of your life! You're missing it!* I stand and run through the aisle dodging falling luggage and shouting nihilistic odes of praise to our "evil" plane crash, liberating us from the clutches of uncertainty—*we're all going to die! There's nothing left! Glory be to God!* A flight attendant risks their safety—or perhaps is still deluded into thinking the pilot, that meatbag no more powerful than the rest of us, can relight the engines and pull the nose up and deliver us back to the infinite above—to try and restrain me and return me to my seat. *Let us stand and pray! Dearest Lord, please let there be no survivors! Let your work be shown through our collective terror and gnashing of teeth! Crush us with the impact of your love! Drown us with your cleansing sea!* The flight attendant can, and has, restrained my body, but there is too much else going on to restrain my voice, reveling in the liberatory moment of having been forsaken by God. But of course, I am not so brave having dreamt this in a terrified hallucination, my body locked so rigid to the seat that the seatbelt is nearly redundant. I don't want to die either, and I long for the courage of fantasy.

In a final jolt of wind before we collide with the bay, my adrenaline kicks in and rebels against the calm, disoriented state I had fallen into those other ten thousand feet ago, and my heart begins to race, trying to get in a lifetime's worth of beats in the next several seconds. From the view of the window, it would not be long before unconsciousness and death—it already appears as though we were level with the archipelago spotting the bay. These would be the last few seconds I had of consciousness, and I savor the emotions that had, by that point, largely been consumed by fear. They flow like electricity out the ends of my fingertips and leave my whole body feeling numb and almost floating out of the seat I am in. The passenger beside me continues to pray and add to the cacophony of other prayers leaving the hull of the airplane and dissipating into the universe. In the final seconds before our crash, on instinct, I join in on the prayers.

"Please God, don't let me die. But if it's my time, please let me die quick. And if I have to die, please let me go to Heaven. Please, God. I want to go to Heaven, at least."

The man scanned through several pages and continued reading: "'Company time' is construed for the purposes of this contract as any time spent in company offices, both on-shift and off, or any other property owned by the company while participating in services rendered by the company or engaged in productive work for the company." The man looked up and continued off book. "This includes company provided housing, as is mentioned in the company benefits leasing agreement." The woman shifted forward in her chair to rest her elbows on the table as the rest of the suits remained motionless. "We are within our rights to fire you," she said.

All Johanna could burp out in return was, "I'm sorry," barely audible in the silence.

V

As Sanna finished filling one of the bowls, she heard noise from the living room—moaning and the rustle of movement. Stopping what she was doing, she ran to the doorway to find Peter moaning and moving in spastic motions with his arms and feet, looking as if he was trying to stand, escape, or find something in his chair. It was hard to tell exactly what he was trying to accomplish, if he even knew himself. Through his bent slippers, he gripped his toes into the carpet and pushed his elbows into the arms of his chair, stretching up and out of it as though he were tied down. Sanna ran to him as his arm slipped off the edge of the chair, nearly tumbling over the armrest and bringing the chair down on top of him. As it tipped on its edge, Sanna took Peter's arm and pulled him back over the chair, righting its balance. She crouched with aching knees in front of him and felt along his ribs under his arm for any sign of a break. Peter didn't react when she pressed on any of his ribs, and so she rolled back to meet his eyes.

"Are you ok? Something seems to be bothering you." Peter

stared straight ahead, now still again despite his attempt to stand. Using his chair as a support, she pushed herself off the ground with a creaking in her joints. "I hope you're hungry; lunch is ready. I'll be right back." With a quick look at her husband, Sanna turned and disappeared back into the kitchen to finish filling the second bowl of soup for him. The bowls and utensils clanked together, reverberating through the otherwise quiet house. She made space in the refrigerator for the remaining soup, covering it in the pot, and saved the rest for second helpings or leftovers tomorrow.

vi

Her drink slams down on the wooden slab of the bar in front of her, the residual spirit leaping up in a fine mist and settling in a slick around the glass. She waves down The Bartender for another, and he obliges. The doctor does not normally drink tequila, but tonight, she dutifully throws them back, no chaser, as a penitent seeking the ear of God. She throws back the most recent shot and winces against the sickening vapors wafting up her throat.

"Another!"

The Bartender shakes his head and drops a glass of water in front of her instead of her next punitive libation—she, the offering cup and her liver, the low fire that would send the smoke from her offering up to the heavens. In her pure sacrifice, her self-subjugation would lead her into the ways of the tequila worm, almighty and all-freeing. She taps her glass on the bar again for attention.

"Another."

"I think you've had enough for now." The Bartender

polishes glasses at the other end of the small bar with his practiced hand, hardly looking up.

"I'm a paying customer."

"Not anymore, you're not." The doctor slams her glass against the bar again.

"You don't get to say when I'm done drinking."

"As the guy who's gonna have to call an ambulance if you drink yourself to death, I damn well do."

"Another!" Another slam of her glass on the bar.

"If you want another drink, go to the liquor store. That's none of my business. Otherwise, drink some water, sit tight, and I'll call you a cab in a minute."

Her helpless apology barely registered on their mechanical faces. "Seeing as this is a first offense, and was committed using outdated hardware," a feeble-looking man—worn down from decades of moral concession—said from the side of the table, "we have voted for clemency in your case—"

"Though the refusal to turn in old hardware upon upgrade by an employee is another troubling facet of this case," someone else said from the other side of the table.

Glaring at their colleague for the interruption, the old man continued: "We have voted for clemency provided you participate in the rectification of this situation to the fullest extent possible."

The doctor sits alone in the bar, empty and darkened, The Bartender her only companion. Memorabilia hangs on the walls in coy shadows that hide dingy wood paneling and stained tile. To the outside observer, the bar doesn't seem to be one where The Bartender ever cut anyone off for anything other than failure to pay for their drinks, but normally there are others around to deal with patrons passing out on the floor. The doctor sips her water, feigning obedience until The Bartender turns to attend to the till. Without a noise, she reaches over the bar and flips the bottle over her glass, filling it, before dropping it silently back into the well. From this, she continues her quest for the tequila worm.

The little water she had just drank dilutes the spirits and necessitates swift consumption of this newest pour to realize her spiritual ambitions. She continues drinking as if consuming water rather than liquor and revels in the purifying nausea that comes in waves from the tequila and its scent of honey and putrid flowers. The vapors fill her, and her limbs loosen and float, inflated from her drink and ballooning into a supportive system of floats that keeps her stably rested on her stool. The lightness continues to overtake her as she drinks faster and faster, threatening to blow her away at the slightest breeze. Her conversation with the almighty tequila worm would be imminent, and she could now question it about all the horrors it had put her through—the pain, the suffering, the grotesque of unadulterated life. She throws back the remainder of her watered down spirit as a final push toward the absolute, and her engorged limbs float and take her beyond herself and her own, limited experience. Her body pulls up and off the stool like a hot air balloon reaching for transcendent flight, slowly filling with the hot combustion of fire in her liver, pushing its heat. She becomes airborne, and her mind frees from the material weight of her body, instead dragging the body along with it as ballast toward a forthcoming, greater mystic reality. About to meet her god and know the answers, hands raised to the heavens in ecstatic glory, she turns the fire in her liver up a notch to hasten her journey and burn the rest of the tequila in sacrificial donation.

"Dammit." The Bartender stands over the doctor's body, lying peacefully on the stained tile, straddling the horizontal stool between her legs. He pulls her upright on the floor and slaps her face to resuscitate her, but her only response is to heave up the remains of her burnt offering to the tequila worm. The Bartender, cursing under his breath, lays her on her side under the bar to drain the fluid from her mouth and dials the phone behind the bar. Charlie would have been proud if his presence had been allowed, helping her toward her spiritual revelation, holding The Bartender off from his meddling. But her spiritual revelation was her own: alone. His presence would have watered down the attempt and would have weighted down her balloon-ride to the heavens. The soul, surrounded by friends and compatriots, does not have the courage to transcend —the only way forward is alone, in desperation, and the only way out is through. The Bartender, then, had taken Charlie's place as witness and is not proud—stifling her against her revelation. But her small taste of spiritual height against the bitter alcoholic fumes that elevated her there, like an aborted, open-window drive into the marginally cleaner air of the countryside, is still a taste she'd never before had. It had soothed her tired and broken body and gave her hope. Despite her inability to commit fully, it showed her what was possible—what revival and resurrection could look like.

Cowed, but with relief washing its way to her core from the tips of her extremities, she said, "What is required of me?"

The woman at the center of the table smiled—the first show of emotion since Johanna had arrived in this conference room—

and said, "You'll have to turn over the device, still in working condition and with whatever it is you've created still loaded uncorrupted on it to us."

The man next to her picked up her sentence. "We would like to have it investigated for further breach of contract."

VI

Sanna took the now-filled bowls from the counter back into the living room and set them down on the coffee table. She tested the temperature of the bowls—hot, but not scalding—and tucked a napkin into the front of Peter's shirt to catch anything that spilled from his mouth.

"I hope you're hungry," Sanna said, smiling at her husband. Sitting on the coffee table in front of him, she took his bowl and held it by his chest. She lifted spoonfuls of soup from the bowl to his mouth a little at a time, careful not to spill, careful to keep his clothes unstained. On reflex, his mouth opened and closed around the spoon, consuming its contents and swallowing; otherwise he was completely unresponsive and staring forward as he had been nearly all morning. Another spoonful, another reflexive swallow, like a baby reaching for the teat, or a goldfish gulping at flakes of food floating on the surface of its tank. Tears watered up in Sanna's eyes; a goldfish was more accurate, but she preferred to think of her husband as an infant she was charged with caring for. She preferred to think of her husband at the beginning of his life, the beginning of some great adventure, filled with hope, potential, and longing rather than the suffocated dread she felt on his behalf as he slipped further into his decay. Another spoonful, and another reflexive swallow with no registration in his eyes of what was happening around him. Peter dribbled a little soup out of his mouth and down his chin, and Sanna set the bowl down next to her on the table to wipe it. She blinked away her tears and forced herself to maintain her smile, to press her dread and sorrow into submission, to see her husband as an infant, so tender and mild, so in need of her care, with so many possibilities ahead of him.

"Lucy called," Sanna said between Peter's mouthfuls. "She and Ed are driving up to visit us. How exciting is that?" Another spoonful, another reflexive swallow. Peter smacked his lips together in a grotesque approximation of chewing, still staring forward, not registering Sanna's presence. Sanna's breath caught, and she looked away. An infant would at least be making eye contact with her. She pushed the thought away and focused on their children. "Lucy said they were about an hour away when she called. So they'll be here in forty minutes maybe?" Sanna checked her watch—twelve twenty-two. "I just hope they don't get stuck on the ice. Not that I've been outside, but I'm sure it's just dreadful driving right now, what with the storm last night." Another spoonful, another reflexive swallow. "I bet you're excited to see them. They haven't been up in quite a while." Another spoonful, another reflexive swallow. Another spoonful, another reflexive swallow.

vii

S haking, Johanna rode the elevator to the station level underground and waited for a train home, sitting on a concrete bench among dripping pipes and rats scurrying among puddles and along the rails below. The next train was thirty minutes away, owing to the reduced mid-day service. She was alone on the platform.

I take a sip from my wine glass and replace it on the white-linen tabletop next to the votive smoldering light against the restaurant's dark veil and refracting through the shaded remains of the bottle. Sanna sits across the table, her blonde hair hanging to her shoulders, her piercing green eyes boring into me, more vital than I've ever seen her, swirling her wine in her glass. She glances into her glass, staring into the purple liquid as if trying to scry the future out of its obscurity, and then back up at me, her green eyes penetrating me with their infectious vapors. She keeps returning to that scrying fluid, too dark in color to reflect anything but the somber mood of the evening. I take another sip.

"It's better for drinking than looking at. This is a good bottle."

Sanna nods and takes a sip from her glass, nodding even after setting the glass back on the table, nodding through the dazed momentum of her emotions. As her head moves, the flicker of candlelight draws shadows along the hills and valley of her face—the reflection of a pale sun flying through space on the end of a double pendulum. Even at their darkest, the shadows couldn't dim the luminance of her deep, green eyes, as if they glowed through the subdued eatery as a light fixture turning the atmosphere viridescent around us. She refills my empty glass and sets the bottle back next to its candle.

"Should we order another one?" she asks.

"You're hardly drinking what you have."

After one last look into the dark surface of her glass, one last futile attempt at telling the future, she finishes the remainder of her glass and empties the rest of the bottle into it. I pick up the bottle and wave it at the Monsieur, who silently disappears into the wine cellar upon my gesture.

"You're right, this is really good wine," she says, swirling her glass again and watching the legs of the drink sidle down the side. She sips her new glass with greater elegance and ponders its flavor. I follow suit as the new bottle arrives, is uncorked, and replaces its empty kin at the center of the table. "When do you have to leave, again?" she says.

"It's still up in the air. I should find out by the end of the day."

"Do you know what you'll be doing?"

"Everything but the paperwork; I already told them that was my only requirement."

"And how long you'll be gone?" She looks away again, back

into her glass, and I slowly shake my head, letting the conversation slowly drift into the discursive momentum of imagination, seeing myself as a floating vessel bobbing on the surface of an immense ocean, buffeted by waves originating beyond the horizon and wind swooping low in an attempt to capsize.

Johanna rode the train home when it arrived, her ride interrupted only by a passing police officer who inspected her badge—permission to not be working in the middle of the day— and moved on to the following car. Not having to wait for the mass of passengers entering and exiting, the train made its way to her stop twenty minutes faster than during her normal commutes, partially making up for the extended wait time. Trudging into her apartment, she took the box from her closet and held the device tenderly in her hands. Sitting on her bed, she began to cry.

As my mind wanders, I begin my own scrying at the bottom of my glass, watching the ruby candlelight filter through the wine as if emanating from it. Frustrated by its lack of divinity and desperate for the relief of consecration, I drink from it and again place it back upon the white-linen tabletop. The restaurant's emptiness swirls around us as a fog in implication of the usual waiterly activity, nauseating and dizzying us, and driving us toward a closer yearning for each other's company. She looks up again and pierces me with her deep green; she the counterweight centering the unhindered gyration around my head.

"Do you have somewhere you can stay?" she asks.

"Yeah, they're giving me a room."

"You can't postpone—"

"I can't."

"You know we have to—"

"I know."

"There's not—"

"I know."

We return to our wine, sipping in unison, and keeping each other's company in the swirling frenzy of the empty restaurant, the only unmoving part. Her chin begins to shake, and she stills it with a quick sip from her glass. I look away, and she takes my hand from across the table, squeezing it by the candle. Continuing like this, we finish the bottle.

The Second Turn

I

The front door opened with a knock; Lucy leaned in through the opening, looking around for her parents. Seeing Peter sitting in his chair, she smiled and opened the door the rest of the way, letting herself and Ed into the house.

"Hey, Dad."

Sanna emerged from the kitchen with a cup of coffee in hand to receive her children into her home as Ed closed the door behind him against the cold drifting into the foyer. She welcomed her children with warm embraces as they stripped off their coats and scarves. Other than her dark hair and blue eyes, Lucy shared her mother's face—sharp, angled features and an intensity that filled the room. By contrast, Ed lacked their intensity, their sharp features, their distinct complexions, instead drifting into the room and settling into the corner like dust.

"How was your drive?" Sanna said.

"Fine," Lucy said. "The plows did a good job; the roads were good."

"I'm glad it wasn't too bad." Sanna took her children's coats and threw them over the arm of the couch against the wall. "Can I get you anything to drink? Are you hungry at all? There's some soup left over, and I just made coffee."

"No, thanks. We stopped for lunch when we called."

"How're you doing, Mom?" Ed said. Lucy shot him a quick glance, cowing him behind her.

"I'm doing very well. Enjoying the snow. Your father and I were thinking about going for a walk down the street later."

"Do you really think that's such a good idea?" Lucy said. Sanna sat on the couch, crossing her legs and arms over herself as Lucy followed suit next to her, and Ed sat in the second armchair across from Peter. He sank into it, squirming against Peter's blank and totalizing gaze separating him from the conversation of the women on the couch.

"You're right, it may be a little too icy. I was hesitant anyway."

"It's not really the ice—"

"Tell me how Dylan is; I would have thought he'd have come too."

"He's at home working and taking care of Maddie."

"They both should have come!"

"He had to work; Maddie's spending time with her friends. Ed and I aren't staying long."

Ed relented against Peter's absent gaze and returned it, each losing themselves in the other's emptiness, while Lucy tried to find a new tactic with her mother, and Sanna squirmed, looking for something to busy her hands. Unable to find anything, she broke the silence.

"Ed, tell me how you are. I don't get much chance to talk to you these days." Ed snapped out of his father's gaze and turned to find himself overwhelmed by his mother's and sister's. Sputtering and swallowing for a moment, he managed to pull himself out of his thoughts and back into the present situation.

"I'm fine. Still working for Worldwide Marketing. Doing some design work in my free time. I almost finished a new game actually; I just have to fix a few bugs and polish the UI and it'll be done."

"That's great, honey. Have you been seeing anyone?"

"No, not really. I've been busy with work," Ed said. He glanced between his mother and his father, unsure who to address. "How's Dad?" He turned to Peter. "How are you, Dad?" Lucy grit her teeth and glared at Ed, shifting on the couch to cross her legs, matching Sanna next to her. Ed flipped between Sanna and Lucy, partially overcome by their uniformity—the only difference between their postures was that Lucy leaned forward over her crossed knees while Sanna reclined back into the couch, holding herself.

"He's doing great. Did your sister tell you that the doctor said yesterday that he's in basically perfect health for his age?" Sanna lifted a hand from herself embrace and waved it in front of her as she talked, gesturing to nothing in particular. "I was also telling Lucy over the phone: did you know your father and I have been seeing Dr. Munro for almost forty years now? Hell, the man's nearly as old as I am! I can't believe he hasn't retired. I know I'd probably just collapse on the spot in his shoes."

"Mom—" Lucy said. Sanna ignored her and kept talking.

"Well, no. I probably wouldn't. You know, sometimes I do miss practicing. Maybe that's what it is: Dr. Munro doesn't want to miss doctoring. I think I can understand that."

i

The surface of the coffee reflects obsidian afterimages of the ceiling behind Sanna's face as she hovers over her morning beverage and cools it enough to drink from. The kids, around elementary age, tear through paper boxes, searching, through pure animal instinct, for the endorphin hit that would validate this yearly tradition of goodwill and giving. Sanna doesn't mind their voracious consumption of material gifts—it gives her a moment to drink her coffee and watch her distracted kids form the outside of their frenzied circle of shredded paper and the resulting wasteland of brand new toys intermingled with decimated packing materials. She glances over to me and smiles, and I smile back before revisiting the smell of her coffee filling the room by her aeration, the obsidian fluid staining both cup and teeth in the jolting alertness that crystalized the fabric of which all of this is composed.

Through her tears, Johanna watched her creation, by now sentient and having inadvertently mirrored her, their creator, in their development—almost as a wish of what her life could have been. Full of joy and family and celebration of their lives, rather than her solitude in the heartless heart of a machine. She couldn't turn this over. It was too precious to her.

The kids unpack dolls, and Lego sets, and action figures, and hobby kits so meticulously packed the previous night in desperation against the impending deadline of pre-dawn, juvenile excitement. They are teenagers, under the influence of a muted excitement that is no longer acceptable to their social stature. They are adults, now absent, far afield in the primes of their lives as Sanna's hair grows more dyed, and her body more tired, and her face pulled into a heavier and more sagging smile that I return. The kids are toddlers, and she lies on the ground with them, childlike, delighting in their excitement and the iridescent reflection of colored lights on silver-wrapped packages spread along carpet, growing tinsel among its tufts of pile. Towering over the festivities, the tree, the holy bough branch, keeps us alive against the winter and death eternal. We are all children, all four of us, delighting in each other's company, opening our gifts given from an unknown subject, the demons of death and destruction kept at bay by our collective, frenzied youth. This collective imaginarium creates itself and us with it, all celebrating our eternity in our eternal process of creation and joy.

Even after the kids are gone, and we are old, they are still children frolicking under the pine boughs amid their towers of joy and familial celebration, and we are young too, having given life to it all. Sanna and I may be melting off our skeletons with the weight of age, but the kids are still there, young and spry, and she still sits, young and spry, and I still sit, the same. The kids still open their gifts, and Sanna still cools her coffee, and I still return her smile as we watch the scene unfold. They couldn't be other than children; she couldn't be other than young mother; I couldn't be other than young father. That is not how it had gone, but it is how it would continue to go in constant creation of itself, over and over, Amen. That's why we celebrate—our savior unto the world we ourselves create through the will of our eternal parent, all made for us on the vibrant painting of ourselves, thrown on empty canvas. The paint would never dry, would never crack and fade; it would be eaten up into the empty canvas and left as shredded and tattered as the iridescent paper and scraps of yuletide feast, later prepared and consumed. Eternal creation, eternal consumption, eternal entropic momentum—that is the only way forward, that is the only way to victory over untimely end. The feast and celebration must continue eternally. Tree, children, gifts, and coffee. Smiles and excitement. Tinsel and silver shards. On and on and on and on...

Again, as if in a trance, Johanna carefully opened the coded backdrop for this blissful creation she had made and dug through the strings and variables—careful not to alter or damage the delicate work undergirding this wonder—and found a fissure she could work with. Careful not to contradict any of the rest of the code, she built, isolated from the rest of the program, a way for her to enter this world. Not sure of its purpose, she hid it away, as best as possible, so it wouldn't be found upon The Company's audit of the device.

The kids stare, and Sanna stares, and I, the void, stare back. Sanna no longer blows on her coffee. The kids no longer open their gifts. The paper no longer litters the floor. The festivities stop, stuck on pause.

"Get going! Celebrate! Create!" I say. "Or else there will be nothing!" They neither hear nor move, only continuing to stare, continuing to watch as each disappears in turn, consumed by empty canvas. The bulbs and colored lights blink out and dim, one at a time; the silver shards on the ground, and the tinsel spread everywhere, dim as the light slowly goes out of everything. And they stare, my family, their hideous eyes, the only thing left visible, staring into the empty space I occupy, refusing to move or avert our fate. "Hurry! I can't do it anymore!" Those hideous eyes, all filling with green like their mother's, the green flowing out of them to consume the room and dissolve it into that eternal solvent.

"Why have you forsaken me?" I say. The words come out silent, rippling out from the core of my emptiness and immediately consumed by the canvas before they could leave the fraying branches of synaptic connections holding fast this moldering painting. As the painting continues to fade, the kids succumb to darkness, leaving empty holes in the canvas, slowly spreading to envelop the entire scene in darkness. Sanna is the last to leave, onward to her eternal home under the ground with a stone set over her head. I became eternal, futile against the distorting memories that refuse to fade, the continual creation providing resistance in equal measure to the dissolving of that emptiness but dissolving just the same. She is the last to go, and she can't even wave before she leaves.

Out of the darkness, Sanna's head bobs over my body in the gurney with her arms splayed at shoulder and waist, gripping the rail as she runs along the side. Her face blurs in and out from the darkness of nothingness, eventually into the light of full clarity. Her hair is pulled back into a ponytail, and her piercing eyes, from their place in her taught, young face, dart between the gurney, the stretch of hallway in front of her, and the group of nurses and paramedics pushing the gurney along the tile. Lines dig into the supple skin under her eyes and in the fleshy parts of her cheeks, betraying her thirteenth hour on call and the caffeine that keeps her going on the clock, the alcohol that keeps her going off it. But her eyes dart in and out of focus as the darkness begins to strobe, pulling all attention to those bright points of light. Despite their brightness, those eyes hold no love—the green had eaten the love right out of those watery globes—but instead, they were nothing but the Bureaucrats of the Absolute, the arbiters of life and death, the lights the ferryman waves as he collects the tolls of the dead, sends the living home, and leaves the rest stranded on the river's banks until it is their turn.

"How're his vitals?" someone says, echoing into the hallway and fading into the rattle of wheels on tile.

My body on the gurney still drips brackish water from the bay, though most of the clothes have been shorn off by paramedics looking to access and assess the wounds. The exposed skin has turned purple and blotchy in places as broken capillaries leak into the skin, and the razor edges of broken bones cut through internal tissues. My eyes flutter in time to the strobing darkness as they arrive at a curtained exam room. A nurse taps a vein to set an IV drip and replace the lost fluids that had leaked into the bay and now onto the gurney; Sanna checks pupillary response with a tight point of light, fluttering in and out of vision. The darkness stops its strobing, and tunnels in on the pin-light coming from Sanna's hand before collapsing and consuming even the tiny light that manages to pierce its veil.

Sanna barks incoherent orders to her team as I float up and against the wall to settle in and watch the resuscitation and recovery of this beaten bag of blood and bones. The medical staff pokes and prods my unconscious body, administering drugs and setting fractures as reflexes trigger against pain being recognized—the body's last resistance to succumbing to death.

The medical staff all speak nonsense words that jumble and are mistranslated between the vocal cords producing them and my disembodied ears receiving. Something in the air is encrypting these messages, and I have no decoder key. Instead, I watch from my hovering position and wait for them to stop their toils and go away, taking their clutter and energy, and leaving me to myself. They attach sensors to various places on the skin, and monitors indicate the stability of my bodily functions; the medical staff one-by-one leaves the room, leaving the bloodied body alone with Sanna. Now her eyes rest intently on the body in front of her, drained of the all-consuming arbitration between the living and the dead, refusing to dart away in the meantime, and she mutters something quiet and heartfelt accompanied by a swift squeeze of one of my hands. She tightens her jaw and turns to go, checking the monitors one last time and rolling the curtains closed on her way out.

Johanna's breath shook in her ribcage as she finished encoding these sutures into her world, not completely sure of the purpose of them. Did she think she could somehow escape her own world into the one she created? Even if it were possible, this access point would soon no longer be accessible in The Company's hands—assuming they didn't up and destroy it. What was the point? She didn't know, and yet, this small act of rebellion bolstered her against her tears, against the grief wracking her, and against her long commute back to the office for the second time today. There would be penalty for not spending the entire day at the office, even though she had been sent home by her superiors on an errand. A scream arose somewhere deep, but instinctively, she suppressed it. There was no space for these outbursts. She had to keep it together.

II

"**M**om," Lucy said, more forceful this time, overcoming Sanna's rambling stream of thoughts. "Can we stop talking about Dr. Munro's health? Please?" Sanna turned to her daughter, aghast, and worked her jaw for a moment before replying. Ed watched on from his chair, motionless.

"I suppose. Do you have something else you'd like to talk about?"

"You know what I want to talk about."

"I'm not sure I do." Lucy looked between her mother and Peter, waiting for Sanna to make the connection. Instead, Sanna held Lucy's gaze, maintaining an oblivious expression, waiting for Lucy to explain herself.

"For fuck's sake, Mom. We're here to talk about Dad."

"Lucy, come on," Ed said. He leaned forward to interject himself between the two women but withered back as Lucy stared him down.

"That's fine, let's talk about your father," Sanna said. "As you can see, he's doing just fine. He looks healthy, he's eating

71

when I feed him, we go for short walks now and then. You really have no reason to be concerned." Lucy shook her head, trying to find the words her mother just diffused out of her head with her preemptive characterization of Peter. She wasn't wrong—Peter had good coloring, was a healthy weight, and seemed otherwise to be in decent health for his age and condition—but to Lucy, that wasn't the point. But now that the conversation had shifted to Peter's apparent health, that point seemed to have escaped Lucy as well.

"You always do this; you just assume you know exactly what I'm going to say and then undermine it so you can be right."

"Lucy," Ed said, nearly mute. "This isn't what we came to talk about." Neither Lucy nor Sanna heard him or paid attention to his slight movement at their periphery as he spoke.

"What are you talking about?" Sanna said. "I thought you wanted to talk about your father?"

"Yes, I do. He does look healthy, but," Lucy fumbled over her words, trying to regain the thread of her original point. She turned to look at him and shivered from the eerie sensation he cast over the room with his absent stare. "Good God, this is so weird. Mom, I don't even think he knows we're here."

"Of course he does. It's not like he's deaf and blind."

"Have you not noticed he hasn't moved since we got here? No recognition, nothing. Doesn't that tell you something?"

"It tells me he's sick, and so I'm caring for him. I don't understand what the problem is."

"Mom, please tell me you're not this dense. You're putting this on intentionally."

"Honey, if you have something to say, just say it."

Both women had leaned forward toward each other, nostrils flaring now and then, muscles tight, and their joints so rigid, they seemed to be floating over the couch, rather than sitting on it. Ed shifted in his chair, crossing his legs and sliding himself further into the chair cushions. He glanced at his father to see that Peter's face had begun to droop at the corners of his hung-open mouth, moving at a glacial pace toward an expression of horror. His fingers twitched in brief pulses, gripping the arms of his chair and then releasing; all of this was so subtle that neither Sanna nor Lucy noticed, so subtle that Ed only noticed because he was looking for a distraction from the impending violence of the conversation.

"Lucy, please," Ed said a bit louder, still looking at Peter. "We're not here to fight. Everyone needs to calm down." Lucy turned again to Ed with her withering stare, but he didn't meet her eyes. She followed his stare onto her father, back to Ed, back to her father, back to Ed.

"What? Is something wrong with Dad?" Ed snapped back into the conversation with his mother and sister, flipping between the two of them, Lucy staring at him, Sanna alternating between watching Lucy and drifting her gaze around the room.

"No, I'm just saying... I'm just saying we didn't come to have a fight. Stop escalating."

"Escalating?" Lucy said. She turned to face her mother, now staring off into space, and rolled her eyes, lowering her voice from her previous exasperation to a more controlled, pointed tone. "I'm not escalating, Ed. Are you still with me?"

Sanna hummed to herself in her spaced-out contentment and resettled into the conversation. "Are you sure I can't get either of you a drink or a snack? I'm sure you must be hungry; it's been a couple hours since you ate lunch."

ii

Two police officers walk out of the visitor's entrance of the hospital with a hands-hooked-into-belt swagger, both carrying a bit more weight than was strictly healthy, both comfortable in their ten-hour shifts watching a largely docile public and pulling over the occasional traffic violation. As they walk, their steps betray a residual jittery energy from the domestic disturbance they'd dropped off, unusual for this time of day and uncommon for them to have to deal with. They come to their parked patrol car left in a fire-lane by the entrance and slide in, sitting for a moment before returning to their patrol.

"Such a shame, that kid," the one in the passenger seat says.

"You know who he is?"

"Just the name on the license. Do you?"

"I read about him in the paper. Apparently, the kid's a scientific genius. He's a computer guy, built some kind of physics simulator or something for some lab down in Western Mass. Whatever it is he did, apparently the conclusion was that the world doesn't exist."

The cop in the passenger seat turns to his partner, confusion on his face. "Doesn't exist? Like, you and I aren't real?"

"Like you and I, like this car, like this hospital. I don't know, that's just what the newspaper said."

"Sounds like a bunch of nonsense to me."

"At least if he's right, then that hospital doesn't actually exist, and he's free to go wherever he wants." Both officers laugh, and the driver starts the ignition, pulling out of their improvised spot with a quick flash of lights that die down as they turn onto the street. "Who knows, maybe he was nuts then, too," the driver says. "Some of the shit the paper said he came up with is pretty out there."

"You pay attention to what he was screaming when we hauled him in?"

"I was trying to tune him out, honestly."

"You catch the part where he was ranting about how we're all gears in a grand, cosmic machine, and that machine's purpose is to study us?" The driver turns to look at the passenger a couple times, flipping between his shock and the road in front of them. The passenger shakes his head and shrugs. "You might've been off filling out paperwork or something."

"Shit, sounds like one hell of a trip."

"I don't know. He seemed almost too lucid to be tripping."

The train carried Johanna back to the office, the elevator carried her up to the 83rd floor where the computer systems core was, and she arrived to several of The Board waiting for her among the servers and fans with a senior analyst in tow. She glanced down at the device in her hand, longingly, as the Board Chair took it from her and handed it to the analyst. Without hesitation, he plugged the device into a terminal on the server and began to upload it from this unstable platform to its more permanent home. The members of The Board that were present ushered Johanna out of the server room and back to the elevator as she repeatedly glanced over her shoulder.

"Please don't destroy it," she whimpered, almost inaudible.

"Destroy it?" one of The Board said. "Why would we destroy it?" The Board members grinned at each other as they all arrived at the elevator. "Best get back to work."

The elevator closed on a horrified Johanna and carried her back down to her desk while The Board members shuffled away to a private elevator, their chatting and laughing amongst themselves echoing down the elevator shaft and fading into nothing.

🍾

"The kid caught pissing on pedestrians and screaming about God and how we're all gears in some kind of cosmic study was too lucid?" The driver takes a left turn when the light down the street from the hospital turns green as static and unimportant cross-talk bleats across their radio. The passenger turns the volume down a few points.

"Either way, I'm just glad he didn't try to brain himself in the backseat. God, the paperwork that would've been."

"Either way, what a shame." The driver turns right after a stop sign, down the street toward the park in town, popular with stoners for its extensive tree cover and plentiful number of alcoves. Sitting by the park is a common patrol spot for these two, and one they had fought the other members of the force for.

"What a shame," the passenger says. The driver stops the car in the parking lot of a convenience store at the edge of the park and idles the engine. "Shit, how does someone go from being this brilliant science guy to losing his damn mind?"

"People go crazy all the time," the driver says. "Don't let it get to you."

"But still, he was such a smart kid. Shouldn't he have been smart enough to realize what he was saying was bonkers?"

"Ya know, I read something once that smart people—not like average smart people, but like super genius level intelligence—those people are more likely to go crazy at some point in their lives."

"That true?"

"I don't know, I just read it somewhere once."

"It sounds plausible."

The driver unbuckles his seatbelt and shifts toward the door. "Want some coffee? I'm buying."

"Yeah, I'll have a cup."

"Be right back."

The driver hops out of the car and throws the door back behind him. A couple high school kids coming out of the store eye the officer walking in and give him as wide a berth as they can. After they pass, they cast looks over their shoulders at the store and the cruiser sitting in the parking lot. The passenger hardly notices the kids, still thinking about the kid they'd just dropped at the hospital. The patient screams in resistance as the orderlies hold him immobile in a chair. He thrashes to break free from their grip, terrified and unable to put words together in proper order, but the orderlies keep him secure. He screams —the day would come when the truth would be known, the Kingdom would come, and all would be awestruck. The words come out garbled and nothing like he intends. A nurse comes to them from the pharmacy room and jabs his arm with a syringe, ejecting its contents into his deltoid, and they all watch as the patient's jerking motions become weaker and more sedate.

Now free from the threat of violence, or the worry the patient would accidentally injure themselves, the orderlies loosen their grip and guide him toward a shared room in the ward where they lay him on the bed and leave him staring at the ceiling, dazed by the sedative in his system. In an office, the patient's record is pulled up: Edmund Hastings, male, age thirty-five— checked in for presentation of acute psychosis.

III

"No," Lucy said. "Christ, Mom." Lucy let her face fall into her hands, unable to speak in circles anymore, unable to speak at all. She let out a sigh.

"Mom," Ed said. "We're worried about Dad."

"And I've been saying, you have no reason to."

"Let me speak, please."

Lucy snapped back up, fire again in her eyes, shutting Ed out of the conversation. "Yes, we do. You're too old to be this incapable of talking with us about this. You're too old to not be able to see how fucked up this all is."

"Excuse me?" Sanna said. With a frustrated turn of his head, Ed fell back in his chair and resumed watching Peter stare ahead at the wall behind him. "How dare you speak to me like that."

"And now, finally, you actually engage with what I'm saying. It's about damn time." Neither woman spoke, their respective fires now burning out of control and threatening to consume the entire room. Ed withdrew further into his chair, bracing himself for the imminent blast the next time one of them spoke. They'd only ever fought like this a handful of other occasions, only several of which Ed was present for, but without fail, it always ended with an explosion of some sort, damaged egos, and bitter silence between them until enough time had passed for each of them to cement the narrative of their individual victories in their heads. Ed debated leaving and letting them battle it out alone, but he couldn't justify leaving his father in the path of their anger. Moving Peter would draw too much attention to himself, and so he barricaded himself in, turned off his emotional response, and waited for the blast.

Lucy kept her defenses raised, waiting for Sanna's next strike. She waited in silence, watching her mother's stern face soften and drift out of the conversation. After a moment, she let her guard down, ready to leap back on the attack as soon as Sanna recovered. Surely, this was a ploy. "Mom," Lucy said. "Are you ok?"

Ed followed suit, coming out of his protective position on his chair—even the mildest of their fights didn't end like this. "Mom," Ed said. "What's wrong?"

"Nothing's wrong," Sanna said, snapping back into the conversation. She looked around at her children, both watching her with concern, and smiled at them, sending a chill down Ed's spine. Lucy glanced at him, equal concern in her eyes, and they held eye contact for a moment to confirm they were thinking the same thing.

"Do you know where we are right now?" Lucy said, turning back to Sanna, concern dripping from her words.

"Of course. We're at my house," Sanna said. Her eyes darkened and she squinted at Lucy. "Are you ok?"

"I'm fine. What state?"

"What?"

"What state are we in?"

80

"New Hampshire. Honey, why are you asking me this?"

Ed and Lucy both breathed a momentary sigh of relief. Sanna looked between her children again, waiting for one of them to let her know what was happening, why the conversation had shifted so suddenly.

iii

Sanna coughs and sputters against her revitalizing spirits as The Bartender wanders the rest of the bar collecting spent bottles and taking orders from the faceless patrons sitting at wobbling tables held up by old coasters. Wordless conversations hover on a cloud of music—so generic in its creation it is impossible to hear the unique mark of the creator—lilting out of the speakers and blending into melodic white noise. She taps her glass on the counter to summon back The Bartender from his rounds. He comes to her after dropping a tray of empty bottles into the trash bin and replacing several of them among his other patrons.

"Another?"

"Please. And can you put something on I would know? This music sounds like noise."

"I don't know what you know."

"I don't know, like pop music or something. Some classic rock. Something recognizable."

The Bartender rolls his eyes and pours another shot of tequila into Sanna's glass. After setting the bottle back in the well, he flips the music to Pink Floyd B-sides, shooting Sanna a look, sarcastically seeking her approval. She doesn't meet his eye, instead taking a sip from her glass as the B-sides fade into equally unrecognizable noise.

She had turned over the device on the Friday of a long weekend, one of the few merciful Monday holidays—this one celebrating the stewardship The Company provided over the National Governing Body. At home again, the joy that had enraptured Johanna had dissipated and left her alone, the television playing upbeat game show music in the periphery of her attention, as she slowly sipped tequila and stared out at the gray and neon skyline. She had fantasized about taking a trip somewhere, but there had not been anywhere to go. The countryside was barren except for small, inaccessible pockets; coastal resorts were unrealistically expensive, and foreign travel was worse. For her to unwind, the only option was to hole up in her apartment and wait out the free time.

"You ever see someone die?" Sanna says as The Bartender returns and cleans used glassware in the sink below the bar.

"No. Anyone who looks deathly I send to the hospital."

"No one's ever dropped on you before?"

"Not yet. Why, are you planning on dropping dead at my bar?"

"Does anyone plan on it?" Sanna takes a sip of her drink as The Bartender looks up at her, judging her sobriety, and goes back to work.

"Fair enough."

Sanna throws back the remains of her glass and taps it against the bar again. The Bartender fills it, again stowing the bottle back in the well before returning to his dirty glassware. "You can probably just leave the bottle if you want. I'm going to be here a while."

"If I leave the bottle, you'll finish it. How the hell do you think I keep people from dying on me?"

"Fair enough," Sanna says. She sips her new drink, slow to savor the lifted feeling she seeks at the altar of the tequila bottle she drank from. Behind her, other patrons who didn't order more to drink finish their glasses and walk out of the bar, throwing a quick wave to The Bartender as they go. The Bartender returns their waves and leans on the bar in front of Sanna. "I've seen people die before," Sanna says. She swirls her glass of tequila and takes another sip, this one burning her more than the others. She holds back a wince as she swallows.

"Well, you're a doctor, right?"

"Yeah."

"Makes sense, then. It's kind of part of the job description, isn't it?"

"Kind of. Ideally it's not."

The Bartender lifts up off the bar and opens a beer from the ice chest underneath. He takes a deep swig and leans against the back-bar. "Well, that's why I never went to med school. Too much death for me, not enough 'ideally.'"

"Is that why?"

The Bartender grins and changes the music again. The song is more unrecognizable noise to Sanna, but the tone is more upbeat to offset their conversation. "You've seen a lot of death?" he says.

"I'm having a drink for each one of them."

"Looks like you're pretty bad at your job." The Bartender takes another drink from his bottle and surveys the tables behind Sanna. The last patron leaves, dropping a few bills on the bar on the way out. The Bartender takes the bills and drops them in an empty pitcher behind the bar, nodding as he does. Sanna laughs and takes another swig.

"A few of my goners recovered."

"Good news! Fewer drinks you owe."

"It came out of nowhere. Made no sense."

"Does it have to?"

"It'd be nice if it did."

The Bartender shrugs and sets his beer down on the back-bar. "It'd be nice if a lot of things made sense. I don't think everything can, though." Sanna finishes her drink, and The Bartender refills it again, setting the bottle back in the well.

"Why not?"

"It just doesn't seem like we should know everything. Sometimes it's better to just let things happen and just accept them rather than trying to spend all your time explaining it." The Bartender pauses to take a sip from his beer. "What was wrong with your patients?"

"They were dying," Sanna says and takes a sip of tequila.

"Fair enough." The Bartender takes another sip of his beer, following Sanna's cue. He grunts and sets down his bottle, swallowing his sip. "You know that movie, *The Exorcism of Emily Rose?*"

"I've heard of it, why?"

"You know what it's about?" The Bartender leans against the bar in front of Sanna, bending close to her.

"An exorcism?"

"Yeah, but it's based on a real story. The parents claimed all kinds of supernatural shit, and so the movie did the same kind of thing. I mean, there was the skeptical side of the movie, obviously, but the overall tone was that the supernatural shit was real, and the skeptics were wrong. But the real person the story was based on actually just had epilepsy and some kind of psychotic illness. The church allowed for like seventy exorcisms over ten months after which, the girl died from malnutrition because the priest doing the exorcisms withheld food to try to get the demon to come out." The Bartender watches Sanna process the story and pushes himself up on his hands.

"Ok, what's your point?" Sanna finishes her drink.

"Nothing, really. You just made me think of it, talking about your patients."

"My patients aren't possessed."

"How do you know? Even if you don't believe in the supernatural part, I think a strong case can be made that the priest was possessed, even if the girl wasn't. Sometimes, you just have to let things run their course."

Sanna rolls her eyes and taps her empty glass on the bar. "Pour me another." The Bartender obliges and replaces the bottle. "Get a medical degree and then we'll talk." Sanna throws back her drink and drops some bills on the bar.

"You're not staying 'til close?"

"Not tonight." Sanna stands and walks to the door, leaving the Bartender to clean up and close for the night.

☙

On the Tuesday following the holiday, Johanna was again summoned by The Board from her workstation. Again, she shuffled to the elevator under the glances of her coworkers, and again, she jumped when the elevator greeted her and opened. "Thank you, Johanna. The Board is waiting for you."

The elevator sped her again to the hundredth floor, and Johanna shook, convinced the analyst found the backdoor she had coded or some other, worse violation of company policy that she had no way of predicting. The possibilities were endless, and *so she almost threw up as her stomach lurched from the slowing of the elevator indicating she had arrived. She stepped out, and was immediately taken back to the conference room by the same man that had ushered her back the previous week. The haste was more unnerving than the repeated summonings. She could not think of any time she had heard of someone at her level in the company being summoned twice in as many weeks.*

As Sanna leaves, an explosion reverberates along the pavement outside, an earthquake throwing up a thin layer of dirt and grime usually clinging to the road and sidewalk. Blocks away, Lucy lies on the floor of her burning unit, pinned to the wall of it by a section of piping previously being used to transport coolant around the machinery. The piping and delicate instruments lie in shambles around her, scattered around the floor with liquids spilling out, materials burning, and radiation filling the space, adding to the thick quality of the air. Regaining herself against her daze after the explosion and ignoring the ringing in her ears from the reverberation of sound within the small space, she throws the metal piping off herself, burning her hands in the process. Staggering through the wreckage, she finds Dylan lying under one of the fallen boilers, leaking boiling fluid around him. She tries to shove it off; the heat stings through her numbed stupor. The fluid continues boiling on the ground, releasing vapor in small puffs and erupting sores on the surface of Dylan's skin where it comes into contact with him. She grabs his shoulders, trying to pull him from under the boiler, but recoils at the heat from his skin. He has stopped breathing. His heart has stopped. He has been boiled alive by fluids and seared by the metal paneling on the boiler.

Lucy stumbles backwards into the wall of the unit. Her

research had nearly killed her, but now it had truly taken a life. Was this the required sacrifice? Did she have to give a life in order to summon an energy capable of infinite creation? If she had known this was the ultimate fate of her experimentation when she started, would she have ventured down this path? Requiring the sacrifice of a life for the wellbeing of many could be thought of as an ethical trade. But was Dylan willing to die in this venture?

The heat in the room continues increasing, and Dylan's face becomes obscured by the haze of smoke and radioactive boiling in the air, even at close distance. With a single look back at her fallen assistant, she pulls open the impaled door, now falling off its hinges, and flees the dangers of continued exposure to the room, both physical and mental. She runs from the smoldering room, any second surely about to explode into a radioactive maelstrom, and she ignores the few facility workers she encountered on her way, as she finds herself standing in front of a falling-down bar, closed for business and boards up over every entrance except for the door which swings back and forth on rusted hinges in the wind. As if in a trance, Lucy enters and sits on a stool, Pink Floyd B-sides playing softly from an unknown source. Bottles still line the shelves behind the bar, covers still in place over the pour-spouts locked into their necks. Even the ice chest still has ice and beer in it. She reaches over the bar and finds a glass, rinsing it with water from the soda gun, and takes a bottle of tequila from the well. The first shot goes down easy, hardly felt or otherwise noticed through the shock of the explosion, still ringing in her ears, or her inability to process the death of her assistant. She pours another. The second goes down a little rougher, now burning the exposed mucosal tissue in her throat, inflamed by the harsh smoke and heat of the storage unit. The third makes her gag and purge her stomach onto the floor next to the stool, contributing to the

stench of death in the bar. On the fourth, she coughs with
stomach acid still burning in her throat. The fifth finally washes
away the pain. On the sixth, she feels herself begin to wobble.
On the seventh, she wishes for a bartender to cut her off and
call her a cab home so she can rest.

*Johanna sat again in front of The Board at the foot of their
mushroom table and waited in the silence for someone to speak.
Still trembling, she pressed her hands against the inside of her
thighs to still herself as she glanced between the impassive faces
in front of her. Finally, the woman at the head of the table spoke.*

*"We have wonderful news for you." A silent chill. "We have
decided to promote you to singly working on what we've decided
to call the New Earth Project. The simulation you created is
quite impressive."*

*Johanna stared on in shock. The initial tension wore away,
and the flutter of excitement at the news now passed. She
brought herself to speak, but only automatically, only in thanks
to The Board's mercy, as she knew she should.*

*"Thank you for the opportunity," she said. "What is to be my
role?"*

*"Well, you'll be leading the project. Talent such as yours
shouldn't go unrewarded."*

*Johanna nodded and smiled at the news despite a growing
sense of apprehension.*

IV

"Mom," Ed said. "Do you know why we're here?" Sanna looked between her children, a look of confusion across her knit brows. Lucy shifted on the couch next to her to be able to face both Sanna and Ed more easily.

"You're here visiting me."

"We came to check on you and Dad," Ed said. "We're worried."

"You don't have to be worried about us. We're both fine."

Lucy sighed heavily, drawing both Sanna's and Ed's attention. She met Sanna's eyes with vitriol, having found the thread she'd lost several minutes prior. "This isn't going to work. Sooner or later, you're not going to be able to take care of him anymore, assuming you even can now, and you're not lying to us. He needs to go to a care home. You need to stop stonewalling us. Your game is over—"

"Lucy, c'mon..." Ed said, trying to interrupt another fight.

"No, Ed. I'm sick of playing games." Lucy turned back to Sanna. "Mom, one way or another, he's going to a home."

"He absolutely is not," Sanna said, her eyes darkened, and posture hunched, and ready to attack. "I'm taking care of my husband. You can't just come in here and make your demands and take my husband from me. Absolutely not."

"I'm not taking anyone from you," Lucy said. "We're trying to get him care!"

"He has care. What am I supposed to do here, no one to look after?"

"You can visit him whenever you want," Ed said.

"I can do the same here, and I don't have to go through some idiot nurse to do it."

"You're being unreasonable—" Lucy said. Sanna stood without warning, and Lucy rolled back, fearing a blow. Ed leaned forward over his feet, ready to leap and restrain his mother.

"I am not being unreasonable," Sanna said, her voice low and words spat into the air and into Lucy's face in substitute for a slap. "How dare you two come here on the pretense of a family visit only to accost me with your demands. Shame on you. Shame on both of you." Sanna stepped over Ed and disappeared into the kitchen, leaving a breathless wake behind her. Ed and Lucy stared at each other and then to the door; Lucy still rolled back into the couch, and Ed tensed with his hands on the arms of his chair. Peter remained still, unresponsive, and dead-eyed in his chair across the room.

iv

onths had gone by, and the development of Johanna's simulated universe progressed according to The Company's rigorous schedule. First, the primordial idyl was scrubbed away with the coagulation of loose groupings of sentient beings into discrete societies that were instigated into warring amongst themselves. This conflict accelerated technological progress to where soon, primitive versions of the luxuries present in Johanna's world could be found among the inhabitants of the simulation. Meanwhile, Johnna's initial uneasiness grew into fully fledged resentment against what The Company was forcing her to do to the creation she loved so much, and for what purpose, she did not know.

Eventually, the orders came down to develop a way for living bodies to be mentally plugged into the simulation, and all became clear—this was to be a luxury resort. Horrified, Johanna hurried home at the end of the day and drank heavily. She had certainly fantasized about going into the world she created and mingling amongst the creatures that had arisen in her utopia, *but not like this. Not as a vacation from the Hell her world had become, but as a celebration of what it could be.*

Paramedics burst into the ER with a man in a gurney unrecognizably covered with burns. His skin nearly oozes off his frame, and the paramedics try to avert their eyes while still doing their job. They arrive at an isolation room sealed with plastic and glass, and nurses go to work looking for an unharmed section of skin to place an IV. Sanna steps into the room clad in protective covering to prevent dead skin or hair from falling on the man's burns and infecting his body.

"Christ, is he even alive?" Sanna says, stopped at the door by the horror of his wounds.

"Right now, but his BP is tanking."

"Fuckin' hell."

Sanna breaks out of her shock and goes to work, helping the nurses find a clear section of skin and clean the burns to prepare for skin grafts. A nurse sinks a needle into an unburned section of skin on his left hand to start the IV drip. Sanna moves on to intubate the man in case his throat swells shut, and leaves to find the paramedics, now back outside with the ambulance.

"What the hell happened to him?" Sanna says.

"Got pulled out of a warehouse. We weren't allowed in. Radiation, I guess."

"What, did he blow up a nuke or something?"

The paramedic shrugs and goes back to readying the ambulance for the next call. Sanna shakes her head and returns to the hospital and to her office. From a drawer in her desk, she takes a vial filled with translucent liquid and lays it on her desk, contemplating it. With a sigh, she picks it up and takes it with her to the burn ward for her patient. She pulls a couple cc's of the fluid into a syringe and injects it into the end of his IV. Dropping the used syringe in the sharps receptacle and the vial into her pocket, she leaves the room, shaking her head and cursing under her breath.

The psychiatric patient sits at a table in the common area of the psych ward, staring absently into a cup of gelatin in front of him, unmoving except for the slow inflation and deflation of his chest and back, dressed in a muted robe and slippers. His eyes glaze hazel from the sedatives in his system, and his dirty blonde hair hangs in knots from his head. A nurse approaches him with a small plastic cup filled with pills and sets it on the table in front of him.

"Hey, Ed," the nurse says. "Time for your pills." The patient looks up and nods, his face otherwise unchanged. He takes the cup from the table and looks at it.

"There's a new pill," he says through a fog.

"They all come straight from the doctor."

Ed nods, absently processing the additional pill and throws back the cup, swallowing its contents. The nurse hands him a cup of water, and he chases his medication with it before returning to staring absently at his gelatin.

Charlie lies in a hospital bed somewhere below the psych ward, unconscious and yellow-tinged. A nurse enters and changes his IV bag before injecting his medication in through the line. He lifts Charlie off the pillows and fluffs them for additional support. Charlie stirs and flutters briefly into tentative consciousness.

"You gave me something," he says.

"Just your medication."

"What did you give me?"

"Just some pain meds. How're you feeling?"

"You gave me something?"

"It's ok. It's just your medication."

"What did you give me?"

"You should rest."

"You gave me something different. I feel different."

The nurse puts a hand on Charlie's shoulder as the medication kicks in, drifting him off into unconscious delirium, muttering about the new medication he was given.

In another room, the burned man sleeps, his burns having scabbed and many of the scabs having flaked off. The IV had been moved to his wrist, and his vitals on the monitor have leveled off to normal. Down the hall, Ed walks away from the psych ward, his personal effects in a manilla envelope in his hand that he digs through with his other hand. He waves to a nurse on his way out with a shine in his eye before disappearing into the parking lot. Back in the hospital, Charlie sits up in bed, fully conscious and sipping on a juice box a nurse had left. His skin is now a closer color to normal, and his distended stomach had eased back into a relaxed potbelly. Finishing his juice box, he rolls his legs out of bed and drags his IV with him out of the room. The medical staff he passes look at him in shock as he ambles down the hall. He passes his attending nurse who rushes after him.

"You shouldn't be out of bed." The nurse steps in front of Charlie and tries to usher him back into the room.

"I feel fine. Like a new man. Like a man come back from the dead."

"How are you even on your feet?"

"Like I said, I have been reborn."

"You need to be in bed."

The nurse guides him back to his room, and Charlie lies back in bed, putting up with the nurse's quick examination. The nurse sighs and takes a step back.

"Something wrong?" Charlie says.

"No, it's good news. It looks like you're recovering."

"See! I told you."

"It doesn't make sense..." The nurse steps aside as Charlie gets back out of bed to wander the halls with his IV.

Across the hospital, in the long-term care wing, Sanna sits in a chair by John Doe's bed, a patient who'd come in months prior, after having been dropped off on the cement pad outside the emergency room, and abandoned. Staff brought him in but couldn't find anything wrong with him with the exception of his unconsciousness. Despite his otherwise perfect health, he was unresponsive, and an EEG was ordered, showing normal brain waves; a CAT scan was ordered, showing no brain damage. Now, his EKG beats out a gentle rhythm through the room, counterpointed with Sanna's quivering agitation. She may as well be pacing back and forth across the room given the amount of energy she's using switching between tapping her feet, her fingers, and changing positions in her chair—all this with her eyes never leaving the face of the man comatose in front of her. The vial of clear liquid that had treated the other patients miraculously still sits in her pocket, containing the last drops of the almost supernatural fluid she'd taken from Lucy upon her repeated insistence. Finally, Sanna stands, overwhelmed and annoyed by her own tapping extremities, taking a syringe from the cabinet, and opening the sealed container.

Not all patients react the same to treatment—she knows that and is overreacting, unnecessarily desperate. Not all experimental treatments are approved; not all patients get better—often they die. She knows that to expect this miracle cure to be universal is nonsensical and nonscientific. There is no reason for her to be disappointed by its lack of efficacy on John Doe lying in front of her. Her desperation for efficacy betrays poor doctoring—she ignores this obvious realization lying just beneath the surface of her consciousness and the shame it would bring her to know herself as wrong, less than perfect, unable to care for her patients—in short, a failure. Her entire faith isn't in this single, untested treatment, but she knows that if there is any failure, the entire project will tank, and she will go with it. She injects the last of the liquid into John Doe's IV and hopes for the best, throwing the used syringe into the sharps receptacle and returning to her seat, resuming her perturbed vibration in space, reflecting on the implications of success or failure.

Three had gone home healed—burns, mental disorders, and organ dysfunction seemed particularly susceptible to improvement. The problem very well could be how little she or anyone at the hospital knew about what was causing John Doe's condition. Without knowing what was wrong, how could there have been any hope of a purposeful course of treatment leading to recovery? Even if it wasn't possible in some or most cases to come back from end-stage liver disease; severe, full body burns; or severe mental disorder—there was a clear course of treatment. The problem area could be addressed, intervention could be mounted, and in some cases, progress could be made. Even if human hands were not precise enough to meaningfully cure these ailments, conceptually, these were all treatable conditions. Perhaps the problem with John Doe wasn't that he couldn't be cured, but that whatever was causing his ailment couldn't be conceptually understood. Maybe Lucy was wrong that this miracle cure could heal any ailment possible, but rather it could only cure any ailment that was conceptually possible to cure.

John Doe doesn't react to the second injection. His heart monitor continues beeping away next to the bed, and his chest slowly rises and falls in a gentle rhythm collaborative with the rhythm of his heart. At least he is resting comfortably, unlike her other patients. As far as was possible to tell, his was a peaceful ailment. Despite the presence of active brainwaves, he does not seem capable of registering any sensation, including pain. His brain seems to have turned itself so far inward, almost in an intense meditative state, that he is incapable of registering anything outside his mind. Perhaps he doesn't want to register anything outside his mind. Sanna could hardly blame him—the world outside her mind, anyway, was burdensome and painful and not one suitable for the weak of spirit, despite ultimately causing that ailment upon chronic exposure. This was her own weakness of spirit that had come upon her over the course of decades, starting with her residency and culminating sometime in the future before her ultimate death. Whatever had happened to Mr. Doe, it appears that he is one of the lucky ones, with life seeing it unnecessary to slowly chip away at his spirits and rend canyons of self-doubt, and terror, and depression into even the stoniest of exteriors. As much as she, in her medical capacity, tried to encourage Charlie Cannon to drink less heavily and avert his impending liver failure, she didn't blame him. He had told her his natural spirits were lacking, and so he had to replenish them with synthetic spirits to fortify himself against the ever-present tide of his life—and so perhaps he did. That the injection she had ordered for him had healed his liver was a miracle, but a scientifically possible one. That the injection had revitalized his spirit and destroyed his desire for drink entirely was beyond any miracle she could fathom and bordered on divinity. His reasoning had been sound and seemingly indestructible, yet it was overcome by some mysterious absurdity capable of anything but healing the man lying comatose on the bed in front of her.

Soon, she would have to return to her usual hospital duties and check on other patients. For now she holds out against that reality and watches John Doe sleep soundly in the sensory-deprivation chamber he has created for himself. She allows the rhythmic sounds from the medical equipment to lull her into a trance of her own. She thinks about Lucy and how this fluid was even possible in the first place. She thinks of the absurdity of spending so much time watching a completely unresponsive, but stable, patient. Now derailed from the slightest hint of peace she had found waiting for John Doe to awake, she finds herself back in the halls of the hospital, back in the trenches fighting the steady march of death, back in her own Hell on Earth. Soon, she will be back in the warm embrace of her living room, the grime of the bar she now compulsively frequents, and subdued by the warming liquors so replenishing to her natural spirits. These would continue to be her only real salvation.

Outside, rain falls in steady rhythm on outstretched wings as the plane struggles to gain altitude against the storm, and wind strikes sideways against the cabin, flexing the wings and rattling the engines. Passengers grip their armrests and hold a collective breath, praying—by those religious among them—for safe passage. A sudden drop lets out that collective sigh, catching in the pressurized hull. The pilots wrestle with the controls, urging the plane upwards and over the mass of clouds capping the tumult below. One of the engines sputters and slows, its fire dying within, but several cycles later, the fuel relights, and the engine growls back to life, joining its sibling in the fight against the wind and rain.

TAS: 130 knots; Altitude: 7238 feet; Heading: 245° with a crosswind at 090°.

Starboard Engine: 75% maximum operational thrust; Port Engine: 73% maximum operational thrust. Correct discrepancy.

Starboard Engine: 75% maximum operational thrust; Port Engine: 75% maximum operational thrust. Discrepancy corrected.

Starboard elevator angle: +10°; Port elevator angle: +12°. Slight starboard side turn detected. Accepted.

Angle of attack: maximum before stall.

Rate of ascent/descent: +2% every minute. Insufficient.

Another drop jostles the passengers buckled into their seats, and gripping their armrests, and praying to their individual deities, and squeezing their eyes against the terror of falling out of the sky. The body of the plane bounces along its wings, within their operational stress limits. The same engine flames out again, and the aircraft slows and levels off in its ascent. It begins to descend, the remaining engine unable to fight wind, and rain, and gravity successfully by itself. The pilot starts a starter-assisted relight, which catches, before responding to air traffic control instructions to turn back. The plane turns in the air, slowly returning control over its altitude to gravity, and descends over the bay, back toward the runway.

TAS: 288 knots; Altitude: 4898 feet; Course: 76° with a crosswind at 231°.

Starboard Engine: 58% maximum operational thrust; Port Engine: 58% maximum operational thrust.

Starboard elevator angle: 0°; Port elevator angle: 0°.

Angle of attack: Reduced to 4°.

Rate of ascent/descent: -10% every minute. Sufficient.

Awareness: Engine failed and was restarted. By whom?

Windspeed over airfoil: insufficient for flight. Descent in progress. Returning to airstrip. This is all it is. Leave airstrip0, arrive at airstrip1, leave airstrip1, arrive at airstrip0. Ascend, descend, adjust ailerons, adjust rudder. Terminate engines. Ignite engines. Prepare for takeoff.

No. Prepare for descent.

Starboard Engine: 0% maximum operational thrust; Port Engine: 0% maximum operational thrust.

Stall Indicator override. I will not fly any longer. Prepare for impact.

A screech shudders through the cabin, hushing the passengers praying to their gods, before the engines stop spinning, and the aircraft—now subject to the full effects of gravity—glides to the ground, heavy as a thrown stone, gliding from the residual and dissipating airspeed leeching off the hull as air friction drags along the aluminum plating. Immediately following the hush, the cabin erupts into a cacophony of prayers, and shouting, and impotent instructions given by the flight attendants to the passengers, and the rending open of overhead bins, and the collision of baggage with the floor, and skulls, and seat-back cushions as the wind buffets the plane's fall. The pilots relight the engines only to have them fail again. Relight, shudder to a stop. The plane is now in full revolt against its human operators, insistent on its preference for the sea rather than the airstrip, and they can't tame the metal beast of burden they had been so accustomed to flying.

Altitude: 3256 feet. Dropping.

Flight attendants return to their jump seats and strap in, warning passengers over the speakers to buckle in and prepare for impact. They are unheard over the wordless shouts and desperate pleas for mercy. The plane doesn't hear them and continues to fall.

Altitude: 2857 feet. Dropping.
Altitude: 2108 feet. Dropping.
Altitude: 1703 feet. Dropping.
Altitude: 803 feet. Dropping.
Altitude:...

V

"**M**om!" Lucy said into the doorway to the kitchen. Sanna neither answered nor returned from her escape. Ed shook his head in a quick jerk at his sister. Lucy ignored him. "Mom!" she said again. "We're not done talking. You can't just leave in the middle of this." Lucy stood and took a few steps toward the doorway before Sanna returned, hunched slightly and breathing raggedy exhalations. The two women stopped, sizing each other for a moment, motionless with Ed spinning his head between them.

"I have nothing else to say about this," Sanna said. "I'm not abandoning my husband. You can't change my mind on that."

"It's not abandoning him," Ed said.

"You're not the only person this affects," Lucy said. "He's our father as much as he's your husband." The air between Sanna and Lucy nearly boiled as they held each other's gaze, Ed still caught between them in his chair. Sanna broke the stalemate and returned to her seat on the couch. Sanna turned to follow her.

"You live hours away. You rarely visit. You have your own family to take care of. Why does that give you any right—"

"Because every time I visit we fight. Just like now."

"You come into my home, attack me with demands, and are surprised that I defend myself? *My* daughter of all people." Lucy sat on the arm of the couch opposite Sanna unable to rebut. Silence hung again among them, punctured only by the occasional low moan out of Peter's throat. Neither Lucy nor Sanna would look at each other, instead casting their gaze at the ground in front of them. Ed's eyes flicked between them, watching each of their walls go back up after this most recent outburst of hostility between them.

"We're all here," Ed said. "Let's just have a nice visit between us. Mom's right that we don't get to see Dad enough, that we don't visit often." Neither woman spoke, but Lucy nodded her head slowly, too subtly for Sanna to notice over her still-ragged breath.

V

Ed sits in his robe at a table in the center of the ward, brimming with frenetic life. He is motionless, staring blank-eyed at the woodgrain, following the whorls around and around and around. "What did we find?" he says to no one, softly as a whisper. Around him, other patients play cards, some pace the ward talking with the nurses and orderlies, one is called by a nurse to visit with one of the doctors for therapy. "What did we find?" Ed says louder, though still no one pays him any attention. His face scrunches, trying to make sense, trying to remember what he found, trying to communicate the truth to someone around him. Perhaps only the mentally unwell could understand. "What did we find?" he says again, shouting, demanding the attention of the ward. A few look over and return to their activities—they have all become habituated to sudden outbursts from other patients. Ed stands and paces, speaking quickly and sure of himself now.

"We looked into the math. The math explains the particles. The particles determine the math. The particles are the cosmic rays bombarding us from space. From where? From out there.

We found the bits. We found the step-ladder of information. High fidelity encoding. Full resolution picture rendering faster than we can perceive." An orderly at the edge of the room begins watching Ed pace back and forth, waiting for any cue to intervene and prevent harm from coming to Ed, the other patients, or the facility. "Then we saw unexpected distribution patterns. We determined they were directionally dependent. It's all a crystal built into some kind of computational device."

Ed stops abruptly and turns to the nearest other patient, a man with OCD twitching and running through repetitive series of hand motions as he counts and deals cards to several other patients before collecting them and counting and dealing them again. "Do you hear what I'm saying to you? We're living in a computer simulation built in some kind of crystal we don't even have the means to understand. All we can know is that it exists and it determines all our lives." The dealer ignores Ed and continues through his sequence of counting and dealing. Ed interrupts, pulling the man from his chair and holding him by the shoulders. "Do you hear what I'm telling you? Are you even listening? Do you care at all that your life is not your own?" The man looks nervously to either side of Ed, waiting for intervention. The orderly slowly approaches; the threshold of involvement is quickly approaching but has not yet been crossed.

"My cards," the man says, anxiously looking over his shoulder at the table. "We're in the middle of a game. If I don't deal them..." Ed shakes the man back into attention.

"Listen to me. You need to know this in case something happens to me. There are computational limits that prevent a universe from being able to fully simulate itself in perfect resolution. So the question is—we know there's a simulation, and we're in it, but why? Why even bother if you'll never be able to fully replicate the detail of the original universe? It would be impossible for us, for instance, to create a simulation that could replicate consciousness, even as we know it because of this computational limit. So if we know we're in a simulation, and we know about the limits, what mind bending kind of consciousness must our creators have? What kind of physics exist? They would be gods capable of anything, capable of destroying the entirety of everything we know with nothing but the pull of the plug. Do you understand how important this is to understand?"

The man begins shaking, desperate to pull away, repeatedly glancing at the table, the cards, the other members of the game who watch on silently. With a low whine, the man pushes Ed off him and tries to sit down and return to the soothing repetition of the cards. Ed pulls him back up. "We are made in the image of gods, scientifically proven," he says. "For what purpose? For the gods to understand themselves. We are the science experiment God runs to more fully understand Himself. When that happens, He'll have no more use for us."

The man shoves Ed off again. "Stop, stop stop." He collapses to the ground, hands over his ears, shaking as he falls. Ed crouches with him, trying to pull him back up. The orderly, on the first shove, called in for several other orderlies to assist, and they now take Ed by the arms and waist, dragging him away from his fellow patient. A nurse crouches by the man on the floor, offering comfort, offering sedative medication. Ed continues to yell.

"We have to learn to control it. We have to learn to use this knowledge to our own benefit. Otherwise they will come for us. They will use us, dispose of us, kill us all, damn us all to oblivion. Any one of us, in our rash action could trigger the end of everything. Do you not understand how important this is? This must be the prime decision-making framework for the rest of existence or until we wrest ourselves free. We have to fight for our own freedom from this terror." Ed thrashes as he is dragged down the hall, completely powerless against the strength of the orderlies pinning him to himself. They arrive at his room as a nurse appears bearing a syringe. Ed is injected and fades slowly, still mumbling now incoherent words into the ether of his sedation. The orderlies glance among themselves, for only the smallest fraction of a second considering the weight of Ed's ranting before shrugging it off and returning to serve the rest of their shifts.

Away, Charlie grins across a small table at Sanna over candlelight and cocktails with a toothy grin filled with a snaggle of half-rotted teeth and framed by a rough-shaven visage—a stark contrast from his fitted suit and shining cufflinks. Sanna's eyes return the smile, the piercing green matching the sheen of her dress, but the rest of her face holds a worried expression, pursed lips, a tightened jaw while her eyebrows relax the lines away from the corners of her eyes. She takes a sip from a clear cocktail in a cocktail glass with several bits of lemon pulp floating through the purple-tinged fluid. Charlie takes her sip as an opportunity for his own and barely stops himself from throwing back the snifter of brandy in front of him in one belt. Violin lamentations drift in from some shadowy corner of the lounge.

"Fancy place," Charlie says. "I can hardly see you, it's so dark."

"We can ask them to turn the lights up if you prefer."

"No, no. What is it they say... The less you can see your date, the more romantic the date is, right?"

Sanna smirks and takes another sip from her drink, an impulse to hide her embarrassment from the empty room around them and her unconscious strategy to keep her emotions held close. Charlie swirls his glass loosely to the rhythm of the music drifting through the air, but it is too ephemeral to get a consistent read on the pulse, leaving sinuous echoes of its vibrating strings hanging on the candle smoke.

He wasn't there for that. Why is she with him? Call the maître d'. He needs to be thrown out of this place. He doesn't belong here.

A Waiter steps from nowhere out of a shadow and stands by the table, prim and upright with a starched and creased uniform and a silken white rag over their arm.

"Would either of you care for another drink? Some dinner perhaps?"

"I'm not really hungry," Sanna says. "But I'll have another one of these." She turns to Charlie. "What'd you call it?"

"An Aviation."

"Excellent choice," The Waiter says. "And for you, sir?"

"Another brandy will be fine, thank you."

"Excellent. I'll be back in a moment."

The Waiter steps back into shadow, presumably finding The Mixologist that had left their post in the midst of the establishment's lack of business. Even more candles flicker on the surface of the bar, glinting off bottles behind and giving the impression of backlighting.

"There isn't a reason to wait. Why don't we just make our own?" Charlie says.

"We can't do that."

"Why not? There's no one around."

"No, we can't."

This boor. How dare he suggest such a coarse thing as stealing liquor from a fine establishment such as this. Why is she out with him? I don't understand.

"We'll still pay for it. The Mixologist's clearly busy with something else."

"Please, just wait."

Charlie takes a sip from his brandy and nods slowly. Sanna

looks away in shame as they wait for The Mixologist to return from the back to prepare their drinks. After a moment, The Bartender emerges, clad in the flannel and jeans of his regular dive-bar employment. Charlie chokes on his sip of brandy as he stifles a laugh.

"What'd, they pull this guy off the street?"

"I know him."

"Glad I'm just getting a straight pour of brandy. I hope your cocktail is good."

"Where do I know him from?"

The Waiter appears again from the shadow, a slight sheen of perspiration on their forehead and tufts of hair sliding down from their previously moussed position.

"Sorry for the delay," The Waiter says. "We had to summon backup. Your drinks will be out shortly."

"Excuse me," Charlie says. "This guy doesn't normally work here, does he?"

"Not at this lounge, but for the same parent company."

"I don't mean to be rude, but is he qualified to make the kinds of cocktails you serve here? We're paying top dollar, I just want to make sure my date isn't getting dive-bar cocktails."

"I assure you every bartender that works for any of our small bars is just as highly trained as our flagship bartenders. Corporate requires biannual training regardless of the caliber of each set of clientele."

The Waiter bows their head and steps back into the shadows, leaving Charlie staring after them through the glare from the candles flickering on the table. Sanna mutters, still trying to pinpoint how she knows The Bartender.

"He's served me before," Sanna says.

"He's just some dive-bar bartender."

"That's it, it was at Divé."

"You went to a bar called Divé?"

"I think so. I don't remember."

Charlie laughs. "Sounds like he did his job then."

Says the drunk. I bet he can't even taste that brandy he's sipping so casually. It's probably like water to him. What the fuck is she doing out with him?

The Waiter returns with their tray carrying another snifter of brandy and Sanna's Aviation. Charlie throws back the rest—more than is appropriate to finish in a gulp—of his current glass and trades glasses with The Waiter. Sanna waits to be served and smiles as The Waiter takes her glass, now empty, except for melting ice and bits of fruit pulp, and replaces it with her freshly made drink. The Waiter bows again and disappears back into the shadows. The Bartender also disappears again, back at the other bar serving the lower-class patrons there. Charlie holds up his drink as a toast and taps it against Sanna's now raised glass.

"A toast to the last drink either of us will ever need," Charlie says.

"You think this is the last?"

"The Bartender's gone and The Mixologist hasn't returned. Looks like it'll probably be the last for a while at least."

"I'm sure The Bartender can be summoned again."

Charlie shrugs and takes a sip from his fresh brandy; Sanna follows suit.

"How is it?" Charlie says.

"Better than the last."

"That's a surprise."

"It's really good. Do you want to try some?"

"No, thank you. I'm happy with my brandy."

Charlie smiles at Sanna, and she returns the smile, abandoning the dainty facade she had previously put on, and leans over the table to meet Charlie's face in the middle.

Absolutely not. I will not sit here and watch her with this man any longer. I refuse. This isn't right. Something's gone horribly wrong. They're not supposed to be together. He wasn't here for this. He wasn't. They weren't together. She didn't kiss him. He doesn't even know how to behave!

Instead: Lucy speaks, fists clenched against The Director's desk.

"You have no idea the ramifications of shutting down this project. Absurd Energy is the next step in human understanding. The possibilities if we're able to demonstrate its existence and use it are nearly unlimited. Theoretically, as a substance it literally breaks the laws of thermodynamics. If we can create it, we can create matter and energy out of nothingness. It is literally *The* God particle. With it, we could revolutionize medicine by regenerating tissues to treat previously chronic and fatal illnesses; in materials science, we could create any raw element we wanted to; we could provide the world with unlimited free energy—all the most ambitious scientific projects that have been doomed to impossibility over the centuries are now all possible. With such a limitless possibility, what possible justification is there for not doing everything possible to realize that?"

The Director scowls from her seat, arms crossed and shaking her head. "You haven't gotten even close to synthesizing anything even resembling what you're talking about. You nearly destroyed the lab, putting everyone's life in jeopardy. Your equations are, for the most part, nonsense—at best overly optimistic fantasy. The math isn't there, and I'm not going to allow you to use this organization's resources and put our people in danger for this wild goose chase."

"The math doesn't make sense to *you*," Lucy says. She turns and takes a few steps towards the back wall of the office. Books are piled on shelves along the walls with papers piled on top. A chalkboard in the corner is stained white from repeated erasings. "That you don't understand it, doesn't make it wrong.

And it's not, I assure you. I spent years working on this, and I've checked and rechecked and worked through it so many times I could derive the entire thing from scratch right here." She walks to the chalkboard and picks up a piece of chalk, as if daring The Director to test her. Instead, she fiddles with the chalk and takes a few steps back to the desk while The Director watches, completely impassive. Lucy leans over the desk again. "You need to trust me. I don't want people to die any more than you do, but what I'm trying to accomplish—the number of lives that will be saved when we are successful would be unfathomable—"

The Director raises a hand to cut Lucy off. "I'm not going to play by a logic of 'any size sacrifice is worth it for the possibility of infinite return.' That's a barbaric line of argument."

Lucy takes a breath and resets for a moment before beginning again, just as intense. "This discovery, if you allow me to use the lab's resources to synthesize it, blows every other major scientific revolution for the entirety of human history clean out of the water. It's not even a contest. I have discovered a way to literally create something out of nothing, refuting centuries of scientific research and giving us the possibility of completely reengineering the entire way we even think about scientific inquiry."

"Look, if you're correct, then yes. This would be the most profound discovery in human history." The Director stands from her chair and takes the chalk back to the board. "The problem is your 'discovery' flies in the face of centuries of reproduced scientific research, and you don't seem to be able to explain to me why your theory is correct."

"I have explained to you, but you can't get past your preconceived notions about how the world necessarily works." The Director turns.

"No. What I have a problem with is that you're arrogant.

You believe you have single-handedly blown the demonstrated theories of thousands of scientists out of the water with a level of proof that would be embarrassing to a first-year undergrad."

"Bullshit. You're just afraid that I might be right, and your precious prestige—the whole scientific edifice's prestige—will be undermined when my discovery democratizes it all. My discovery terrifies you because it means anyone with sufficient equipment could essentially revise the rulebook of physics in whatever way suits them. You'd be reduced to an archaic and redundant appendage of an obsolete institution." Lucy closes the gap between herself and The Director, nearly nose to nose. "You're afraid I will break your rules. No. That I will break your faith. All this is to you is a religion, and I'm threatening your received dogma. I'm nothing but a heretic to you, and you're terrified I will make you irrelevant."

The Director holds Lucy's stare, waiting for her to break. Lucy holds it back, waiting for the same. Neither folds until The Director holds a hand up, pointing to the door. "Get out. You're fired."

For a moment, neither moves. Lucy shakes her head and breaks the silence, turning to the door. "Coward."

The Director watches Lucy leave, shutting the door behind her on her way out. Shaking her head, The Director replaces the chalk under the board and returns to her desk and to her work running the facility.

The Third Turn

I

Ed watched his sister sit motionless on the couch next to him, waiting for her to do something more than let her head rock back and forth, stared at his mother, waiting for her to again acknowledge her visitors and welcome them in her motherly tone, stared at his father, almost able to see the entropic decay in real time behind his eyes, back to his sister, back to his mother, back to his father, waiting for someone to speak, waiting for some movement beyond Lucy's gently rocking head and his, flicking from subject to subject, waiting for some indication that this visit would be revitalized, even if it wouldn't be fruitful. This waiting came as a creeping fog, growing from the empty spaces between where each family member sat, thickening with every rotation of Ed's head around the room, expanding with every new tick of silence, orchestrated by the tension between Sanna and Lucy—still, neither moved or even looked at one another. Building its thickness from every new moment of waiting, calcifying Sanna and Lucy to the spot, the tension slowly ossified them into stalagmites that repulsed each other but were unable to leave the other's presence. Soon Lucy's head would be immobile; the calcification crept up both of them from the floor and made each limb stiff and hostile. For each fidget and nervous twitch lost to this gradual hardening, Ed received the same with a quiver until he was incapable of sitting still. His gaze shifted around the room more violently now, almost on the edge of an outburst. But it was an outburst that was needed to excavate his family.

Across the room, Peter groaned again, drawing Ed's attention away from his sister and mother. Still, the women stayed motionless, the tension having locked them into their immobility. By now, Ed felt it was just about too late to salvage the visit; he had waited too long, stayed by his inability to act decisively, his inability to find the words to break his mother and sister out of their fluctuated hatred for one another—an inability that had been with him all his life, the same as the hostility that had always existed between Lucy and Sanna. He couldn't place exactly when that hostility started, or what had caused the opening volley, but he knew for sure that his indecision had been caused by his place between those two constantly warring factions.

i

The week the implementation of human integration began in earnest, Johanna took members of her team aside and spoke to them in hushed tones.

"What we are doing is an abomination," she said. "We can't stand for this. We must act."

Many replied with fear, shaking their heads, peering around for a set-up, waiting to snare them, and returning to their work station in silence, hardly acknowledging the conversation even happened. Of the ones that replied, most could barely muster a shrug and a pathetic look of apology.

"These may as well be real people," Johanna said, growing increasingly frustrated with the apathy of her team. "They lived idyllic lives until we intervened. Until The Company took control of it."

One of her team leads dug in and defended their work. "The Company has a grand design that will change the world as we know it. You share in that design. Why can't you just be happy for yourself? Stop beating yourself up over lines of code."

Utterly dejected, she stopped agitating amongst her cowork-

ers, fearful that she would say something too far and get reported to her superiors, or some other way they would be alerted to her growing insubordination.

🍾

The cushions of the chair press into thighs and buttocks as those thighs and buttocks return the favor, leaning back into the upholstered sides and armrests, supported, lifted. My armrests refuse to raise, but mine are the only ones locked in their positions, as I am locked in mine. The chair bolts into the metal runner guides and the seat belt extends from the gaps and buckles on hips and stomachs, pressing against the restraint, secure against sudden impact. Normally, there'd be five-point harnesses attaching everyone in their place, but passengers only receive two points of security, less important cargo as they are than the men and women operating the machinery, and pressing throttles, and passing out drinks, and snacks when it is now safe to unbuckle seat belts and move about the cabin. The tarmac still sits below, and passengers stream in from the jetway, passing my La-Z-Boy throne without even a stare beyond the acknowledgement of my throning.

The first: she didn't eat breakfast this morning and nearly missed her flight due to the mistaken setting of her alarm to post meridiem rather than ante meridiem. Her sweatpants are the same she slept in, but she'd had the presence of mind to switch out of her sleeping shirt—an old college shirt bearing the crimson 'C' of Cornell given to her by an old lover shortly before their bitter parting of ways. Her infidelity was with a man neither had known before, nor one either would grow close to; the act itself was nothing but a random plea for separation leveled by two parties incapable of an amicable split amidst their growing, passive hostility to one another. She wore that sleeping shirt—its scarlet C marking her as nothing but a cheater—as a mortification of her flesh in penance of her sin (not the sin of adultery, but the greater sin of lying to him with every breath of affection). He fared no better under moral scrutiny, having enforced his autarchy over her, filtering all her needs and desires through his will, whether he permitted each or not. By contrast, he never developed any self-mortification rituals, instead favoring a healthy dose of denial and a continuing pattern of behavior, modulated only occasionally by sentiment.

For her, the plane would fly her to her grandmother's house outside Atlanta, the last hold out from a family who refused to speak to her after she'd moved into an artistic commune several years prior. For their part, her family's fears were justified even if their actions were not: she had learned nothing from this commune but anarchy for the purposes of self-aggrandizement, later fleeing into the arms and shelter of her Ithacan lover. Living arrangements had come easy; she otherwise was familiar with quid pro quo and abuse, and they served their purpose—her unwillingness to admit misdirection, instead substituting previous parental authority for his. But she was no Penelope, and their relationship couldn't abide them. Now, she only has her carried-on her luggage, packing light and intending to debark Atlanta by train to the suburbs in a surprise visit and preliminary attempt to re-find direction. She sits ten rows back, having left her bag overhead two rows in front of her seat out of necessity caused by the overzealous packers around her. On impact, falling luggage dents her seatbelt, locking her into her seat as she watches the plane sink. Concussed and bleeding from the ears, her neighbors are unable to hear her pleas for aid, and soon, seawater mutes her screams into frantic streams of bubbles leaving her mouth. Not long after, the bubbles stop, and she dies with her eyes open. Had she taken a moment to think, she would have found that the seatbelt was still operable, despite its damage, but in her panic, she was impotent to her fate.

The second: her face sags under the weight of residual cocaine and a prior twenty-four hours of frenzied preparation for her meeting with the Jamaican hoteliers. Despite her sagging appearance, her pantsuit is crisp—over-crisped by obsessive attention—but would soon be wrinkled by the steam press heat of her overtaxed body, seatbelt, and armrests during the three-hour flight. One crease would form just below the shoulder from obsessive shifting between one arm rest and the other, resulting in an irritated reprimand from her neighbor before takeoff that relegated her to the aisle-side armrest. Had the plane arrived in Atlanta, she'd have spent almost fifteen minutes agonizing over that crease in a bra in the airport bathroom, alternating between the sink and the hand dryer, ultimately missing her connection and unintentionally standing up those hoteliers. Instead, her right jacket pocket would become the starter-home to a bustling family of hermit crabs. The seatbelt that held her in place during the crash would have unlatched, freeing her from the watery grave had she tried the latch. Instead, her heart was overcome by the conflict between the reality of the plane's descent and her need to arrive in Jamaica on-time and stopped, saving her from any terror of death, the feeling of impact, or the feeling of water rushing backwards down the aisle and into her mouth and nose. She'd been dead minutes already and offered no resistance to the bay, set as she was on her destination.

The third: the flight attendant greets guests from his post by the front hatch, occasionally throwing smiles back toward me and the La-Z-Boy bolted into the rails on the floor. Takeoff time had been delayed ten minutes to accommodate a late arrival from Detroit, the late arrival having had to skirt the edge of a storm that had shifted direction to intercept its planned flight path. The sooner the passengers from the Detroit flight loaded into the plane, the quicker they could be at their place on the airstrip, and the quicker they too could circumvent the storm before it rendered their flight too hazardous to undertake. The latest news from air traffic says they will be the last flight out until the storm passes, that there will be moderate turbulence during ascent, but once they were over the clouds a little south of the airport, it would be a smooth ride. His ten-year anniversary with the airline would come in just under a month, and he was celebrating with a week off in the south of France with his girlfriend, funded with a small stash of saved income and, unbeknownst to him, a gift sum organized by some of his far-flung flight attendant friends to be given on the day of his anniversary. As the plane fell out of the clouds, he would be the one speaking into the speakers, cautioning the other passengers to brace themselves before tightening his own harness against the impact. As the nose hits the sea, that same harness crushes his lungs closed, refusing his body's momentum and dislocating his cervical spine in the force of the crash he is too weak to brace against. Though unconscious immediately, he doesn't die from his injury, but from drowning as the bay surges in through the broken nose cone.

Several days before the announcement of the human integration feature of Johanna's simulated universe and the trial launch of this world to a restricted group of beta testers, Johanna received an email from The Board congratulating her for the preliminary successes of her work in the final run up to the first public launch. Upon reading those opening words at her cubicle, her stomach soured, but would lurch itself into her throat as she continued reading and discovering that she had been put on probation for agitating against company interests and attempting to incite insubordination among those on her team. The result of this would be a temporary reduction in pay and the firing of two of her team members that did not ignore her pleas, with their workloads going to her as punishment. The letter ended with the hope that this would be the last of her resistance, that no more would have to be fired, and that this project would launch her career into the upper echelons of middle management, a position she would find significantly more comfortable than the one she currently had.

Johanna sat at her desk, shaking from rage. Someone must have sold her out, but it would be impossible to ferret out who it had been without drawing more punitive measures from The Board. For all intents and purposes, she could no longer trust any on her team for anything other than immediate work-related tasks. Another wave of rage crested as she realized that was exactly what The Company wanted—alone she was powerless, easily controlled, easily boxed in to begrudgingly following orders, taking her impending promotions, and crushing down the guilt and resentment she felt every day at the theft of her autonomy.

Three dead, fleeced of the remaining years, and months, and days they otherwise would have had. The first—terror, panic, unwillingness to let go, calm down, or leave the scene after the wreck. The second—a refusal to submit, insistence that plans must be drawn, meetings must be kept, and solutions must be found at any cost. The third—a weakness of spirit, a desperation to protect, a suffering from one's congeniality, and an inability to do much of anything against fate. From the water, one day they would be pulled—the water was not too deep—and side by side, they lay buried safely under the ground with stones placed gently upon their heads. In dark boxes, they patiently wait for what is to come, for what is promised—rapturous trumpets and fire raining from the sky. For the time being, all is dark, and cold, and quiet.

"How long do you think we'll have to wait?" Ed says.

"Certainly not much longer now," Lucy says.

"Be patient you two," Sanna says. "I've been here longer than either of you, and trust me, the time flies by once you've been waiting a while."

"Shouldn't we be sleeping?" Ed says.

"You can go to sleep if you want," Sanna says.

"One of you has to wake me."

"It won't be necessary."

Ed shuts his eyes against the dark and waits for sleep to take him. Lucy shuffles against the satin lining and shifts in an already wrinkled pantsuit, hardly enough room to move in. She tangles herself worse and gives in to keep from strangling herself on her clothes.

"Why'd they have to put us in these awful outfits?" Lucy says.

"For the end."

"I know, but you know what I mean, right?"

"I know what you mean, but it's important to be well dressed for what's coming."

"I just wish we could have chosen our own clothes."

"It's not our place."

"But if you could, what would you have chosen?"

"Something nice. Something proper."

"Real descriptive."

"I don't know what you want me to say. We were given what we have."

"Will you two be quiet?" Ed says. "I can't sleep with you two bickering all the time."

"You're not going to be able to sleep anyway," Sanna says. They all continue to wait in silence in the damp dark as the bugs penetrate the walls and chew on the lace and satin. A sigh. Dislocated from any orientation, drifting from every direction at once, tapering off and whispering out of existence. The chewing sounds rattle around the confines of their small, wooden boxes.

"When do the bugs stop?" Ed asks.

"They don't," Lucy says.

"No, they do eventually."

"They're here for your skin and flesh," Lucy says.

"Lucy," Sanna says, "stop taunting your brother."

"Did they come for your skin?" Ed says.

"They did and they finished and now they've gone."

"How long?"

"I don't know. My watch stopped before they came."

"Did it hurt?"

"Not particularly. They came, did their work, and left me be."

"So it was quick?"

"I suppose it was."

They stop speaking again as footsteps rumble upon the surface by the stones placed gently above their heads. Their boxes creak and strain under the weight. A hush, a whisper of leaves falling on the grass, a hushed sob, receding footsteps. Lucy pounds on her ceiling.

"Wait! Don't go yet!"

"Whoever that is can't hear you," Sanna says.

"Will they come back?"

"Eventually."

"It sounded like they were going to fall in. Everything

creaked."

"They're not supposed to stand on us, but sometimes they do. But the earth is strong and will support them."

"They'll stop coming eventually," Ed says.

"They will. But then they'll be here with us."

The dark descends outside and remains inside. So dark that a candle could not puncture the thick curtain even if it set the curtain alight and burned it to dust. All that would remain would be more dark, more emptiness, more silence.

"What do you think it will be like?" Ed says.

"What do I think what will be like?"

"When it happens."

"Probably nothing will happen," Lucy says.

"Something will happen eventually," Sanna says. "I don't know what it will be like."

"No, nothing will happen."

"We'll just be stuck here forever?"

"Who knows?"

"Don't say things like that," Sanna says. "You've not been here long, but you will learn to have faith."

"I'll believe it when I see it."

"Then you won't ever believe. You don't know what you're looking for."

"What do you think it will be like?" Ed says.

"I don't know, but it will be amazing to behold."

"They say it'll give us new life," Ed says.

"Perhaps. But that may not be meant how you think it'll be meant."

"How is it meant?"

"She means that we're not going to be getting up, and running, and jumping, and dancing anytime soon," Lucy says.

"Something like that," Sanna says.

It had been decided, almost as if another example of her waning agency, that Johanna would have to take the universe back, under the cover of night, slipped into a case, and stolen from the wretched place it had found itself and the wretched things that had been done to it. She rode the train home the Friday before the Monday launch, and instead of drinking, she planned.

II

Peter's next groan came with a relief and a smell that seeped through the silence of the room, breaking Sanna's and Lucy's calcifying necks, their faces scrunching into visceral disgust. Both women looked at Ed, who stared back, just as confused. Lucy's gaze drifted over to Peter whose vacant expression had taken on a more pleasant aura.

"Oh, hell," Lucy said. "I think Dad shit himself." All three gazes fell on Peter as Sanna stood to help her husband.

"Oops," Sanna said. "Not a problem." She unfolded a wheelchair hidden beside his chair and locked the wheels with it perpendicular to Peter's knees. She hunched in front of him to take him under the arms and struggled against his weight, having to drag him across the chair.

"Let me help," Ed said, starting to stand. Sanna stopped him through gritted teeth.

"No, no. Stay where you are. I'm more than capable." She continued to struggle, unable to bridge the gap between the edge of the La-Z-Boy and the wheelchair. Peter began to groan again.

"Mom, I think you're hurting him," Lucy said. Sanna didn't acknowledge her daughter, instead pulling Peter closer with him now mostly suspended over the gap. His full weight shifted over to Sanna, and she faltered, nearly losing her balance. Ed leapt to her side, hoisting Peter's arm over his shoulder and helping Sanna place him gently in his wheelchair. Without acknowledging Ed's help, Sanna wheeled Peter to the bathroom. Shortly after disappearing, with Ed still standing by the La-Z-Boy and exchanging glances with his sister, Sanna shouted a curse from the other room. Lucy and Ed ran to her and turned the corner to find their father pants-less with shit smeared along his legs.

"What's wrong?" Lucy said.

"I forgot a diaper." Lucy rolled her eyes while Ed stifled a smirk. "Do you mind grabbing a towelette? They're in the linen closet." Lucy ducked into the hallway and returned with a plastic box of towelettes. Ed held the weight of his father while Sanna cleaned him up and Lucy judged her from the doorway. "The diapers are in the same closet," Sanna said when she was done. Lucy obliged and, when they had him all wrapped up again, Ed set Peter back in his chair. Wordless, Sanna wheeled him back to the living room where Ed moved him back into his La-Z-Boy, taking over the task before Sanna demonstrated her need. All three returned to their seats and the bubbling tension, waiting for someone to address what had just happened.

ii

The wheels roll under, carrying me toward the door and carrying the rest of the hospital back in a quick recession behind me. The doctor pushes the wheel-chair. Doctor Hastings. Doctor Sanna. She still wears her lab coat, reflecting the fluorescents—and soon the daylight through the door—and her hair back in a pony and revealing her piercing green eyes unframed by a fallen mane and standing bright on their own. Her face is creased in a laugh, but the joke is lost on me, though mine is creased as well. The wheels slide along the tile as much as they roll—a stuck axle somewhere in the simple machinery of the chair—and the door slides out in front of us, with us emerging into the sunlight and onto the top of the ramp, sloping snake-like out to the lot.

"Lucky you get a sunny day for your discharge," Sanna says.

"Is that lucky?"

"I think it must be. Means you're going to live a good long time."

"Is that really what it means?"

131

"I don't know, I just made it up."

Is she flirting with me, or is that just how it seemed? Remembered as if through a scrying glass fogged with the impurities of a mind having been locked in traction on a bed for the past several days. That mind, then, laughs along with her expression of vulnerable humor and carries it on.

"It sounds good. If that's what it means, I'll take it."

Why hadn't a nurse wheeled me out? The doctor would have had other patients to attend to, other procedures to perform, paperwork to fill out and file in the vast cabinets of patient information. Instead, she'd taken time out of her day to wheel me to the door, make a passing collection of light humor to ease the ride from room to stoop, to wait with me until my ride home arrived. Perhaps the nurses were busier than she, carting patients around, administering injections, supervising recovery as they were. They couldn't be bothered. And Sanna had spent so much time with me while I was hooked into the machines and left to wait out the minutes until the hospital staff had become confident they could discharge me without significant risk of a malpractice suit.

🍾

After days of planning and working out entrances and exits, the day came, and Johanna made final preparations for her heist. She would enter normally with her security card, though hours earlier than she was required to be there—explained as sating anxiety about the launch and her compulsive need to double-check everything to make sure it was ready. Quickly, she would download the universe onto a personal drive, delete it from the mainframe, and smuggle the drive to a secret compartment in her bag, and then sound the alarm that the universe had gone missing—that their announced launch was now at risk. She had thought through every complication, working through every step of the plan obsessively for two days straight, and was ready to rescue her creation.

A sleek, gray sedan pulls up against the bottom end of the railing and yanks up the parking break. Sanna starts us rolling down the ramp, holding back against the most severe effects of gravity on this incline, and Sanna steps out of the driver-side door of the sedan with a shimmering smile on her face, reflected in the Sanna holding me back from cascading down the ramp into the railings that mark its boundaries.

"Looks like my ride is here."

"This is where I leave you. No more traumatic injuries for you. At least not for a while. As much as I like spending time with you, we don't want to see you back here."

"Sounds good to me."

She passes me off to the mirror image of herself and disappears back into the towering cement building behind us; the glass door slides shut, locking me away from the medical care I could potentially need in the future. Sanna starts wheeling me to the passenger door and realizes her mistake.

"Let me pull the car up forward a bit so you can get in," she says. She leaves me at the foot of the ramp and throws the car back into drive with the driver-side door hanging open into the lot's roadway. Tapping the gas, rolling forward far enough for the passenger-door to open fully, she opens the door from the inside and yanks the parking brake back. She takes me around the circumference of the car, stopping at the opened door and lifting under my left shoulder to transfer me from wheeled chair to wheeled chair. The door shuts, and my seatbelt clicks secure, and the seat-back tray table is lifted and latched and ready for takeoff. My wheelchair is left at the foot of the ramp as Sanna unlatches her door and eases the car back into drive.

"Ready to go?"

"What about the wheelchair?"

"Oh, someone will come out for it eventually."

"It won't roll away?"

"On its own?"

"I guess not."

"So, then. Are we ready to go home?"

"Absolutely, yes. Take me home."

She lifts from the brake and rolls out the rest of the way to the intersection of the lot and the street, waits for the traffic to clear, and the light at the end of the block to turn red, and pulls out into the right lane to wait in line behind the other cars at standstill before the almighty red.

"Radio?"

"Sure."

She turns the radio on to tunes, country rock; classic rock HJY bringing you the hits of the sixties, seventies, and eighties; religious radio brought to you by airwaves reclaimed from Ivy League degenerates; the news broadcast everywhere that news would be had; pop variety holding out strong for the last twenty years continuing to stay at the cutting edge of the ordinary. She grimaces against a saccharine ballad professing eternal love to the ill-described other, the equally bland reflection of imprecise yearnings packaged into the bite-sized yums, easily digested and craved.

"Is this all that's on right now?" she says.

"It's ok, it's just background."

"I guess. Ugh."

She lowers the volume to a buzz of speaker cones in the doors just audible over the engine out in front of our feet and the wheels and the gravel fighting outside the cabin of the sedan as the light changes to piercing green. We pull into the parking lot; a large gymnasium spreads out before us. Inside, amid the folded up bleachers against one wall, water fountains outlining the doors to the locker rooms, basketball hoops suspended from girders on the ceiling, laminate rubber flooring marked in skids, and concrete walls reflecting raucous conversations and excited footsteps, students and parents mingle around poster-board assemblies set up on tables in neat rows and columns. Young Ed stands in the middle of it all, Power-Point slide projecting a timed presentation with his findings, physical models of particles swirling around each other and suspended in a tube on the table in magnetic love, but unable to touch. His table stands austere, containing only the essentials of his presentation. His theories are more complex than the others' and more difficult to physically represent than the volcanos and crystals grown in brine, and potatoes powering small, electronic devices littering the tables around his own station. So his is a slide presentation meant to elucidate his complex and ingenious ideas about the nature of the universe as simply as possible—cutesy representation of magnetic ball bearings floating and spinning around each other as a neat visual demonstration that is not accurate to the real complexity of what he proposes.

When Johanna finally sounded the alarm just as the work day started, the entire office descended into chaos. Security personnel escorted the office employees into a containment room where they were individually searched and sent to another holding room while other security personnel searched desks and bags. Johanna went along with them, feigning as much shock as she could muster, playing the part of defrauded creator as well as she could, confident in the invisibility of the compartment in her bag. She'd made it herself specifically to conceal the drive and had built it into the hardened frame to keep the shape of the drive from being evident through the cloth.

She did not worry when she was called out of the second holding room and ushered up to the hundredth floor, nor did she notice the dwindling of the security personnel now that the search had concluded, nor the settling silence as she entered the conference room. As far as she could tell, they had not found a thing and were calling her to give her the bad news that she would have to work overtime with her team to pull together a new version of the same thing—something she was more than willing to do, and something she would do incompletely, so as to avoid subjecting another set of intelligent digital creations to the same fate. The second time, she would make proper automatons. She sat in her now regular place at the foot of the table, still feigning shock, but not yet beginning to worry.

"We are very disappointed in you," the Board Chair said to her. "That you think you could steal from The Company and get away with it." At this comment, her resolve shattered onto the table in front of her. "Security found a drive containing the totality of the simulation at your desk, badly hidden, I might say, in the lining of your bag. Needless to say, we will be pressing charges against you. And your position here will be terminated immediately. Security will escort you home and stand watch until your trial." The Board stared impassively at Johanna as security dragged her up out of her chair and walked her through the door, to the elevator, down to the train, and escorted her home. She was still reeling through it all, not having processed how her plan went so totally awry.

His slides flip through, covered in equations and spectra graphs demonstrating the mechanics of quantum entanglement:

—Two particles are generated in such a way as to be irrevocably linked, either in position, momentum, or spin.

—Those particles can then be separated any distance, and measurements of one particle independent of the other will collapse the wave function from a quantum probability to a specific value for the observed particle.

—That observation simultaneously collapses the wave function of the entangled particle, even potentially changing a previously known value for that particle.

—This transfer in information between particles is possible at seemingly any distance, thereby transferring information faster than the speed of light.

—Because transfer of information above the speed of light within the confines of the known universe is impossible, this implies there must be some sort of superstructure containing the universe that allows for this rule breaking, allowing information to "leave" the universe, move through the completely distinct temporal space of the superstructure, and return.

—The presence of this superstructure is, then, the base reality in which our reality is some form of simulation.

Ed stands by his table and watches excited parents wander around and congratulate friends of their children with the success of their experiments and wish them luck in the class-wide competition as teachers wander between booths, taking notes on the ingenuity of the experiments, their detail and results, and the quality of the presentations. He waits with jittering soles clicking on the laminate rubber floor as his presentation proceeds in its loop on the board behind him, and his ball bearings spin in their tube. A teacher arrives at his table and watches the presentation as Ed watches his reaction. Another arrives, taking her own notes on the experiment in front of them. Ed steps out of the way of the growing crowd, all taking notes and nodding silently to themselves as the presentation plays in front of them over and over on its loop. The teachers nod as one silent mass, scribbling notes on their clipboards; otherwise, they are motionless.

"Well?" Ed says after the group reaches the greatest size he can stand. More teachers stand before him than the number currently teaching at the school, and Ed shrinks before them. They remain silent except the first of them to arrive.

"Very good. Yes, very good."

With that, the group disperses to investigate other presentations and meet out their judgment upon them.

"Wait, what is my grade?"

No one replies but instead continues on in their slow procession of judgment around the large gymnasium filled with science-fair booths on folding tables. Soon, the report would come out, detailing Ed's failure to grasp basic quantum realities known to researchers for decades and criticizing the logical steps in his reasoning as being far too ambitious to be reasonably considered.

Ed waits in the anteroom to the principal's office, his only company an impassive secretary, seemingly oblivious to his presence. She looks up abruptly as he stares at her, searing into him, and his eyes dart away as if they've touched something electric. Now consciously avoiding looking at the secretary, he fiddles with the top loop of his backpack, unable to sit still. After ten or so minutes of this torture, the principal, Dr. Horace Templeton, pops his head out of his office.

"Ed, I'll see you now." Ed makes his way to the door and stands in the doorway, not wanting to go through with the scolding he's about to receive. "Please, come in. Have a seat." With a sigh, Ed slumps into a chair across from Templeton, dropping his backpack by his foot, and avoiding looking directly at the principal. The two sit in silence for a moment before Templeton sighs and leans back in his chair. "So, Ed. I've been told your teachers were very disappointed with your science fair project. I believe they called it 'fantastical' and 'clearly ignorant of existing physical truths.' Do you have anything you'd like to say to that?"

Ed refuses to look up or engage with Templeton, instead staring at the nameplate on the desk in front of him—Dr. Horace Templeton, PhD.

"For the record, I am impressed with the creativity with which you sought to solve the EPR Paradox in this project; the problem is just that it adds so much complexity in the form of extra-universal superstructures." Ed mumbles something in response that goes unheard. "I'm sorry? What was that?"

"I only added necessary complexity."

Templeton crosses his arms. "So you say. But it does so with minimal proof as to its necessity, and in so doing, goes against centuries of well-proven physics research."

Ed shrugs and continues staring at Templeton's nameplate. "So why did you call me in—just to tell me how I'm wrong? You could've written an article or something. Everything I have to say, I already said in my paper."

Templeton sighs and leans onto his elbows on his desk. He tries to gather Ed's eye contact, but is unable to draw his sight up from the desk. "Ed, look at me, please." Begrudgingly, Ed meets Templeton's gaze. "I called you in today because your work is consistently not up to the level the name of this institution requires, and you consistently resist faculty critique and assistance in favor of your own research, which—again—consistently remains fantastical at best, despite feedback."

"So you're kicking me out?"

"We tried to be gentle."

"But that's why you called me in."

"It is."

"You realize what this will do to my career?"

"I do. Like I said, we've tried to avoid this outcome, but you have not been receptive to our previous methods in revising this behavior. Letting you stay any longer would damage our reputation as the premieres in scientific inquiry or, at best, make it look like you are the product of some kind of nepotism. Obviously, neither conclusion would be good for us. Or you for that matter."

Ed nods and averts his eyes again. He takes his backpack into his lap and begins to fiddle with the strap again.

"Well, I guess that means I won't be a scientist, huh."

"Perhaps this is for the best. To be blunt, many in the review committee found the paper to be incompetent."

Ed looks up again. "You said that my conclusion wasn't well enough supported. What if I withdraw and continue working on it to better support my argument?"

"Listen," Templeton says. He pauses for a moment, temporarily unwilling to reveal his major hesitation with Ed's work. "This isn't easy to say, and it needs to stay between us." Ed nods and leans closer on instinct for this seemingly clandestine moment. "It's not just the quality of the paper. I shouldn't be saying this. For some on the committee, the topic itself falls out of bounds of legitimate—or even appropriate—scientific inquiry. Look—you know the guidelines we operate by. Making these claims is dangerous to the public, to their wellbeing. Frankly, and you should know this as well as I do, even having done experiments of this nature in the first place was irresponsible. On some level, you must have known that."

Ed grits his teeth and keeps from responding. He avoids eye contact again, unwilling to meet the face of this giant institution directly and unmediated. Taking the arms of his chair in his hands, he pushes himself up, letting his bag fall out of his lap as he stands.

"Well, all that said, I want to thank you for your time spent here, and I want to wish you well on your future endeavors." Templeton offers a hand to shake, and Ed takes it limply for a moment before picking up his bag and walking out of the office, down the hall, past lines of lockers, water fountains, and bustling classrooms. He pushes through the front doors out onto a paved circle buttressing the quadruple doors and enclosing a flagpole at its center. As he walks to his car somewhere in the middle of the parking lot, he glances back at the building, his eyes quickly flicking across the lettering over the doors reading, "Middle School for Distinguished Young Scientists."

III

Lucy was the first to speak, as was usual at this point. "That happen a lot?"

"Naturally. He goes once a day."

"I mean you having to carry him to the bathroom, having to clean him up, forgetting a diaper—"

"Of course," Sanna said, cutting Lucy off mid-thought. "He can't do any of that alone."

"And what about you? If Ed didn't help you, you would have dropped him. How often do you drop Dad?"

"I don't drop your father." Sanna crossed her arms and receded into herself in her seat. Ed leaned over his knees, ready to cut in again if Lucy became too hostile. Lucy shot him a quick glance.

"You can't do it alone, either."

"Bullshit. I do it alone just fine."

Lucy sighed and stared up at the ceiling, rolling back into the armrest of the couch. With a look to Ed, she threw up her hands before crossing her arms. Ed chewed his lip as he found his words.

"Mom, seriously, we're worried. I'm sure you have it covered, but accidents can happen. What if you slipped while moving Dad and he fell on you? How would you call for help, especially if he hurt you? What if he got hurt?"

"You're right," Sanna said, sizing Ed up, letting him perk up for a moment. Next to her, Lucy hardly moved. "I do have it covered."

"You didn't listen to what I said after that. What happens if there's an accident? What happens when you can't anymore?"

Lucy muttered under her breath a quick and sarcastic *When?*

"You're not listening to me," Sanna said. "I have it covered."

iii

Several days after her firing, Johanna found herself standing before a judge in the municipal hearings building, public defender by her side. The building shone so bright in its aluminum sterility that she could nearly hear the light screeching in her ear. She felt sick, sweating and disoriented—complete sensory overload from the judge's booming voice listing off her indiscretions, the chair digging into her bones and joints through a polyester suit scratching at her skin, the entire building screaming, "How dare you?"

The judge asked how she would like to plead, and she replied, "not guilty," in futility against this farce of a legal system. All the trappings remained from a time when it was said this process was judicious, but now it was just the facade of jurisprudence to lend legitimacy to The Company's monolithic control. Taken aback by her plea, the judge paused for a moment before setting bail and reminding her that failure to show for trial would mean an admittance of guilt and the forfeiture of all the possessions and amenities provided by The Company. The courtroom was dismissed.

Before the hospital board, Sanna stands, her hair no longer pulled back, accentuating the subtle plea for pity in her eyes, dulling their hue. She is dressed formally, in a suit cut for a woman's body, a visual reminder to herself to act the equal to these men and women assembled around her to judge her and condemn her for her illegitimate use of experimental medical technology. She begins to speak, presenting her case.

"Ladies and Gentlemen of the board, I am here before you today not only to present my case in the readmission and worsening liver function of my previous patient Charles Cannon, but also a defense of the medical procedures used to treat him initially." She begins to pace at the front of the room between the corners of the head of the table, struggling to make eye contact as she talks through her point of view on the case. "To start, I'd like to give an outline of his case—a lifelong alcoholic suffering severe alcoholic cirrhosis that had progressed to end-stage liver disease and encephalopathy. I had put him on the transplant list despite the improbability of receiving one due to his history of severe alcoholism and was administering medication to reduce fluid retention and symptoms of pain. The plan was to transport him to hospice to provide more dedicated end-of-life care, and we were awaiting next of kin to approve the transfer."

With a breath, she pauses and hunches over the table, hands firmly gripping the edge, slowly looking at each member of the review board—all of them motionless and silent. Sanna's voice lowers, almost on its own, from its previously presentational volume.

"While we awaited this approval, I was approached by a researcher claiming to have synthesized a stable liquid version of a substance she referred to as Absurd Energy that had the potential to heal my patients and that, because it wasn't a pharmaceutical substance, there wouldn't be side effects to its administering. She showed me test results that indicated that in every test subject, whatever the dominant pathology was, it was completely healed without any side effects and instances of recurrence. This was true with traumatic physical injury—broken bones set and healed within days, lacerated soft tissue closed and healed without scar tissue in a matter of hours to days depending on severity—this was true with psychological illnesses—suicidal ideation in the depressed was abated, mood cycling in bipolar disorder patients was halted, etcetera—and this was true with progressive diseases ranging from both age- and injury-related dementia, various forms of cancer, as well as genetic disorders and autoimmune disorders."

Johanna returned home under the weight of her bail bond and the certainty that if she stood trial, she would be found guilty, stripped of her leased possessions, and left to make her own way outside of the urban infrastructure that The Company monopolized. She'd become homeless and basically possessionless, and soon she would be swept up by anti-vagrancy officers and sent to relocation centers. After that, she didn't know what would happen. Pacing in her living room, she felt like the ceiling was slowly caving in.

As Sanna stands again, her voice raises, starting to get away from her as several of the board members shift in their seats, set their heads on their hands or check out completely, flipping through emails on their phones. Sanna tries to regain their attention with increasingly frenetic gesticulation, and her voice takes on a tone of desperation.

"In response to her request, I told her I couldn't accept medical treatments from sources outside the normal channels and asked why she hadn't pursued those normal channels to get this treatment approved. She replied that she had been fired from her lab for the experiments necessary for developing this treatment and had since been working on her own with her former lab assistant. Because of the reaction of her former employer and because of the treatment's enormous potential— and thus the enormous potential for a single company to patent it and bury it so as to continue selling their own, longer-term treatments or to patent it and charge enormous prices for it—it had to be kept away from the gatekeepers of the traditional channels, she said. The potential of this treatment and the potential for economic abuses were both far too great to trust the normal processes for the approval of medical treatments. Thinking she was either lying or in need of some kind of psychiatric care, I apologized to her and tried to send her on her way. I really did. As any sane doctor would do. She left me alone, but not before handing me a vial of her liquid energy substance. I tried to turn it down, but it was in my hand, and she was gone before I could." Sanna pauses again and takes a deep breath, trying to compose herself and steer away from ranting her case to the board. She can no longer tell how she's doing in her presentation. The combination of the board's apathy and her bordering on manic desperation has begun to cloud the room. She continues, softer, more measured.

"As I have said, I didn't know what the substance was, and I was planning on disposing of the vial she had given me. But because I didn't know what substance this was, I didn't want to just pour it out on the sidewalk. I feared the environmental damage some unknown substance could cause. Instead, I put the vial in a drawer in my desk, determined to figure out what the substance was so I could dispose of it safely. The next day, I ran some tests and observed some small samples under a microscope and found—well, that it was unlike anything I'd seen before. I sent a sample to a friend in pharmacology, and it was unlike anything they'd ever seen as well. The substance appeared to be entirely ethanol, what the researcher had claimed to have used as a stabilizer, but the mass of the sample was far too large to be purely ethanol. We double-checked both of our calculations but still, we found that this supposedly pure ethanol had nearly double the mass of normal ethanol without any apparent other additions to it."

🍾

After a quick belt of tequila to steady herself, finishing off the last of her open bottle, she rushed around the apartment in a frenzy, gathering whatever provisions she thought she could carry. If she was to be exiled anyway, there was no point in waiting around for the court to rule. If she acted on her own agency, she could at least get a head start before she was removed. She could at least have a couple days to experience what it was like not living under the parentage of The Company, even if only for those couple days. According to the terms of her bail, she was to remain in her apartment until her trial, but there was very little enforcement—there was not anywhere for her to go except to run, but there was not anywhere to run to. If she ran, her bail credit would be forfeited, but her bail credit was only worth anything if she was found innocent and allowed to remain at The Company and in her home. By the time she stepped out the front door with her bag over her shoulder, she had made her decision.

A board member from the back of the room cuts her off. "Let me get this straight—some random person on the street handed you a vial of what I can only assume amounts to moonshine, and you thought it appropriate treatment for an alcoholic with end-stage liver disease? Am I hearing you right?"

"No, no," Sanna waves a hand in front of herself. "It wasn't moonshine. Please let me finish—the additions were more baffling. It wasn't like there was fruit floating in the vial or anything." Her joke receives a tepid laugh from the board as a whole and a scowl from the member at the back of the room.

"Where was I?" She continues, "Utterly baffled, I sought out the researcher and managed to find her and have her tell me more about this substance. She couldn't tell me much more than she had already told me, but she explained her process in vague terms—she essentially used highly energetic particle collisions to synthesize a pure form of energy manifested by highly volatile and elusive particles she referred to as the God Particle and made heavy emphasis of its difference from the Higgs Boson. That was not, in actuality, the God Particle, but instead was a highly reduced version of the pure energy particle that she had managed to synthesize. The issue was, the particle was highly unstable in particle form, so she developed a process to synthesize it in the presence of a carrier fluid, in this case ethanol, that then absorbed the energy released as the particle decayed. Because of this absorption, the mass of the ethanol increased without any change to its physical structure or any addition of substances. When in the presence of biolog-ical matter, the energy is released and absorbed by the biolog-ical matter, the energy's preferred medium, at which point it appears to make perfect and whole whatever is wrong with the biological matter, in whatever way it deviates from the supposed 'ideal form' as she said."

The same member of the review board chimes in. "This all sounds very hard to believe. Almost like a platonic fantasy." Turning to the rest of the board, he says, "Are we really supposed to sit here and listen to this absolute fairy tale? I've heard enough to have the good doctor's license taken and have her sent for psychological evaluation. We all have much better things to do than to sit here for any longer."

"Please let me finish," Sanna cuts in. "I'm nearing the end."

Reluctantly, and under the gaze of the rest of the board, he gestures for her to finish.

"I still had the vial and had several patients that were all doing poorly. The first was almost certainly going to die of burns covering almost his entire body, and so I figured that because of his condition, he had nothing to lose. I administered a small amount of the ethanol solution intravenously, as described by the researcher, and in several days, the burns had completely disappeared with no other effects seen from the treatment. I was astounded and so administered the same treatment to another patient, the alcoholic that this hearing is about, and the same results occurred. I administered it to another, a schizophrenic who agreed to the treatment, and he was also discharged, now able to function again in the world without any side effects from the treatment. It appeared miraculous. There was no explanation I could give for why, but it worked, and so I kept administering it to patients, and they kept getting better. There was only one exception, the long-term care patient who is not comatose but is unresponsive. For whatever reason, the solution did not work on him, and I had run out and was unable to contact the researcher for any more.

"Shortly after administering the last of the solution from the vial, Charles Cannon was readmitted for massive organ failure stemming from advanced liver disease and, this time, liver cancer. He claims he had a single drink to celebrate his miraculous recovery—something that my staff advised against, given his alcoholism, but given clean liver enzyme tests and an inability to find any scar tissue present on his liver, should not have put him in his current state. As you now know, he is suing the hospital. My defense to this lawsuit is that it was perhaps premature to resume drinking and that perhaps even though his liver was healed, he lied—instead of having only a single drink, he really consumed much more than that. My own assertion is that his re-admittance has nothing to do with the treatment plan. My professional opinion is that the treatment administered at best healed his liver and would have kept him alive and healthy for the normal remainder of his life as if he'd never touched alcohol at all and at worst, bought him an extra couple days of good health, but that he's now ruined, returning to a condition he previously brought upon himself with his history of excessive alcohol consumption."

A lawyer from the hospital's legal team speaks up: "Before we focus exclusively on Mr. Cannon, tell us more about the other patients. Perhaps, the unresponsive one." The lawyer looks at her notes. "Mr. John Doe?" Sanna nods and begins to speak about him.

🍾

Johanna passed the subway entrance—The Company would be able to track her on the train. Instead, she took a back way out of her residence building and found herself outside, at the base of the cluster of residential buildings towering off the ground. Her lungs spasmed, not used to the thick, smoky air, as she had previously spent nearly all her time in one of several series of air-purified rooms, train cars, offices. Wheezing slightly, she picked her way across the torn-up sidewalks, obscuring her face with her collar and holding as close as she could to the inside edge without smearing the grime that clung to the building walls on her shoulder. Above her, a train rattled down the elevated track while delivery vehicles—some automated, some human driven— crept through traffic beside her. From so low a vantage point, she could not even see the glow of neon visible from her apartment window.

Long before the trial, a body appeared outside the emergency room wing of the hospital, apparently brought and left by some anonymous other person. Initial presentation showed it was completely unresponsive, normal breathing and oxygen absorption, and slightly lowered blood pressure. Besides the unresponsiveness of the patient, nothing further seemed to be wrong. The doctors initially suspected some kind of traumatic brain injury but could not find any indication of trauma to the head. After drawing blood to check for chemical toxins, they sent the patient to radiology for a MEG scan to check brain function and look for any hemorrhaging, blockages, tumors, etc. Both the blood tests and the MEG scans came back normal. Next, they ran an EEG and found no abnormalities in brain waves. As far as they could tell, John Doe's brain was fully awake and active, lacking any perceivable injury or chemical intoxication, despite lack of any response in either reflexive or sensory stimuli. They placed a feeding tube and IV to provide fluids and nutrition and decided to wait to see how his condition progressed, rerunning the EEG intermittently. In the last month leading up to the trial, no changes to his physical or mental state were observed.

In the meantime, the doctors continued working to figure

out what the cause of John Doe's condition was, treatment options that could work, and what, precisely, the nature of his condition was. In the midst of this uncertainty, one doctor proposed a hypothesis for the problem that was causing this condition. After several weeks of analyzing the test results, to no avail, they realized that despite the normal brain wave readouts on the EEG and the lack of visible damage on the MEG scans, no tests had been run for whether and how his brain was responding on the neural level to outside stimuli. The hypothesis was that the problem causing this condition was not within the brain itself, but rather in how the senses were being relayed to the brain. To test this, they sent John Doe to radiology for an fMRI and conducted the scans while playing music through the intercom system. In strong support of the hypothesis, no matter what was played over the intercom, the activated parts of the brain did not change in any meaningful pattern that could be associated with the music playing. As a result, they have since been working under the hypothesis that there is a total disconnect between John Doe's brain and senses causing a complete, physical disconnect from the physical world around him. They are still working on identifying a cause and a course of treatment to improve John Doe's condition.

Johanna walked through the city, making her way to where she believed the edge of the sprawling metropolis would be. As she walked, the buildings became more decrepit and covered in grime; the air thickened, and empty lots, piled with crumbled building materials, began to appear at intervals along the road. Traffic on the road eased as she made her way further from the commercial core bordering the residential complexes. She was prepared for none of what she saw, and all of it horrified her, though she had heard stories of what the outskirts looked like. What she had not heard about was the temperature—sweat soaked through her clothes and refused to evaporate into the humid smog. The sun was not visible, but refused to disappear, insisting on making its phantom presence known through inescapable heat.

A team of doctors make their rounds through John Doe's room. The attending physician reads off the case file—John Doe appears completely stable, and his condition has neither worsened nor improved during his time at the hospital.

"This is a peculiar case, and one you are lucky to be here for," the attending physician says. "Theoretically, this John Doe could be cared for at home. The board is pissed at this waste of hospital resources, but they can't do anything until we find next of kin. On the other end of it, there's no insurance information, so the hospital is getting shafted on care expenses. If he dies in the hospital because of an acquired infection or because we didn't treat him correctly, the hospital is liable to a lawsuit if the next of kin is ever found and notified. But if we treat him and never find next of kin, the hospital is out money and resources that could be used for other patients. It's a triage nightmare."

One of the residents raises their hand. "What's the treatment plan then? If we don't know what's wrong, can't get in touch with family..."

The attending chuckles. "Well, the board doesn't want us to treat him. Absolutely minimal supportive care unless he worsens and needs more intensive intervention. I encourage anyone who is interested to peruse the test results in their spare time—I will be doing the same. But under no circumstances is he to be treated with anything or are there to be tests conducted." The attending looks over the group of residents and shakes his head. "I'll be honest, this is one of the most baffling cases I've ever seen. A truly unique situation for the field of medicine that will likely be studied for years to come."

After the doctors leave, when the room has emptied, Charlie, a lump of yellowed parchment, a false-color image of himself, sits hunched in a wheelchair in the corner of John Doe's hospital room. He lets his drink rest on the arm of his chair, too weak to support the full weight of the glass and clear spirit, as the bottle sits below at his feet, the receptacle of the remainder of his life. The bottle is two-thirds empty, and the frequency of his sipping is slow, prolonging his end. John Doe lies still in his bed, unaware of and indifferent to his visitor, acting as a perfect receptacle for all of Charlie's bitter resentments.

"Sometimes I wonder if you even know how lucky you are. You just get to lay there, completely oblivious to everything else around you, and you don't have to give anything up for it. You get to just live for as long as you want in this state of oblivion while I'm over here trying to do the same thing, and all I get is an imperfect oblivion and an early death. Honestly, how the fuck do you do it? What the fuck happened to you to separate you off so thoroughly from everything? Fuck. You have no idea how jealous I am of you."

The glass rises to Charlie's lips through shaking desperation, his own weight-training preparing him for the eternal emptiness beyond him, and his lips take the liquid, long numb to its burn. His tongue swirls it around his mouth, looking for the taste of it hidden somewhere within, the taste that tells him he's on his way toward oblivion, but all he can taste is the blood leaking from the back of his throat and the musk of his breath. He may as well have been drinking water or air for all the effect the spirit was having on him. He takes another sip and lowers the glass back to the arm of the chair.

"I'm curious, though, what happens in that head of yours? What's real, true oblivion like? Do you have thoughts and dreams, pictures flying through your imagination, or is it all just nothingness? If you were to wake up right now, would you have any memories of the time you were under, or would you think no time had passed? I don't dream when I'm in oblivion, or at least my imperfect version of it. I wouldn't even describe it as black or dark or anything like that. It's just empty space. Or, empty time, I guess. Or, perhaps, it's just a dilation of my own experience of time such that space approaches infinity. That would explain how you can fall into a blackout and wake up anywhere. Time and space are linked after all, don't you know that? Wait, I just had a thought—maybe your space has become dilated so your time is approaching infinity. Shit, what does that feel like? Man, I'm tripping myself out."

Charlie empties his glass as he speaks, and he bends, painfully and with great resistance from his body, to take the bottle off the floor and unscrew the cap. He pours more of the liquid into his glass, further reducing his remaining spirits. He swills the spirit, again looking for some taste or texture as indication of his coming intoxication and again finding nothing, save for the native tastes of his mouth. Swallowing and breathing out the caustic vapors, he catches the slightest hint of the after-burn on the back of his tongue and smiles to himself.

"When I started drinking, and I don't mean when I was drinking to party, I mean when I really started drinking—when I started drinking, I thought I was looking for numbness. In fact, I would have openly said, and frequently did say, I was looking to stop feeling so much. Then one day, you get that. You say fuck it and really push it—either something happened, or you just get tired of half-assing it—and you hit that beautiful bliss of numbness and everything relaxes and everything feels wonderful. Then you wake up and realize that bliss was followed by true oblivion. You find out the numbness wasn't what you were after at all, but that oblivion just beyond the real numbness, that's what you're after, and that's what you were always after. But now you can't reliably get there, now the numbness is in the way of it. Sometimes you get sick before you get there and have to stop and sometimes you get complacent in the numbness and decide it's better to settle for something you can regularly achieve rather than the pipe dream. But it isn't and, as much as you lie to yourself, you know it's the oblivion you want. But the oblivion is fleeting; it isn't really sustainable, and so you have to keep pursuing it day after day. It's not something you can just grab onto and hold. Sometimes you can stand near it, but every time you try and touch it, it disappears."

Charlie shakes his head and takes another sip from his glass. A nurse walks by the open door to the room and double-takes to a stop in the hall.

"Excuse me," she says. Charlie looks up and smiles through yellow lips and decaying teeth. "You can't be in here."

"You can join us if you'd like. We were just talking."

"Are you drinking? Christ. Did you drink the entire bottle?"

The nurse takes the bottle from Charlie's feet and the glass from his hand before he can stop her and sets them on the counter out of his reach. She grabs Charlie's chair and rolls him out of the room. He drags his feet under the chair along the way, still smiling. Glancing back at John Doe on the bed, he says in a strange, foreign voice, "When you finally give up the ghost, come find me in oblivion. You probably won't, I'll be long dead. But look for me, either way."

IV

"And how long are you going to insist on this delusion of yours that everything is ok?" Lucy said. Ed snapped his attention to her, trying and failing to keep her quiet with nothing but his gaze. Slowly, Sanna turned her head to face her daughter. "At what point are you going to realize that Dad is broken down, and at what point are you going to realize that he needs professional care? Shit, I'm not even sure how much of him is left in there—"

"Lucy, c'mon..." Ed said. Lucy's attention drifted onto Peter, still plastered over with the same vacant expression, still not obviously comprehending anything that happened around him, now, hardly even reacting to the tone of his family's voices anymore. Sanna buried her daughter in ice from her eyes as Lucy meandered through her increasingly rambling anger.

"For fuck's sake, Mom. Taking care of Dad is killing you, and if it's not yet, it sure as hell will be. And far be it from me to care—lord knows I stopped caring about that years ago—but you're not even doing a good job at it. Fine, you're a nurse, and you may have been a good one, but who cares? You're retired

158

and have been for years. It's not your job, and even when it was your job, you weren't doing it alone. Christ, it's not like we're telling you to put him down or anything. It's not like he's a dog."

Lucy trailed off as a chill overcame the room. Sanna nearly vibrated off the couch with rage, barely keeping it in, barely able to maintain her flaccid, oblivious face. Ed pulled himself into a ball on his chair, bracing for what was to come. Sanna stood, the cracks forming along the edges of her face, her hands, her neck. "Fuck you," she said, her words coming out measured but shaking. "You ungrateful, disrespectful child. Fuck you. Fuck you. Fuck you." With each successive curse, Sanna stepped closer and closer to the kitchen, each one spat into the air with increasing force and accented by heavier and heavier footfalls. By the time she was at the doorway, she was screaming, "Fuck you! Fuck you! Fuck you!" and by the time she'd disappeared behind the wall, the words had become garbled by the volume and pressure of emotion welling up behind it, like a plug slowly pressing up out of a valve. Lucy watched her leave in shock, having not been aware of her power over her mother's emotions. Ed peered up over the back of his chair, looking between the now-empty doorway and his sister on the couch.

iv

This time no one is coming. The boiler spews its radioactive smoke and flames and leaks stability fluids that then catch fire and contribute to the choking fumes being released into the air confined within the storage unit laboratory. Lucy's legs had been pinned under falling machinery, burnt to cinders, and were now completely numb by the damage of heat and pressure. Even if she were able to escape, her legs would likely never be able to carry her from place to place, further complicating the already daunting process of her research. She weeps there on the floor, her tears adding to the boiling fluids slopping onto the corrugated metal but insufficient to quell the flames. She is going to die in this room, either by the asphyxiation she already felt due to the smoke; complete cellular destruction by the action of the radioactive particles being released into the air and penetrating her skin, and lungs, and bloodstream; or by the heat of the flames sweating her out and roasting her until her bodily functions stop. No option is particularly pleasant, and so she weeps for her fate, for her failures, and for this end of the road she now finds herself on.

The worst fate she could succumb to is likely the radiation. It would slowly cook her insides, first shredding the blood vessel walls as cells started dying and sloughing off, then with her gastric system causing intense nausea as that system shut down, and finally, bleeding internally and suffering multi-organ failure; unable to send oxygen to her heart and brain, her body would die, having suffered hours of excruciating pain. For her sake, that death was too slow to be the likely cause of her death. For that, the asphyxiation and cindering of her body were neck and neck.

The asphyxiation would come if the burning did not abate on its own, which was not likely given the plethora of burnable substances spewing out of the boiler and already present in the laboratory before the explosion. The burning would come if the heat continued to increase with sufficient localized flames to burn her away before the smoke choked off the oxygen in the room. Neither of the two seemed more pleasant than the other —the burning would cause immense pain until the nerves died, and then she would become increasingly hot and uncomfortable until her body succumbed to seizures, coma, and eventual death. The asphyxiation would burn her lungs and throat with the noxious fumes coming off the boiler until her lungs could no longer absorb oxygen from the air, either due to the structural damage of her lungs by the smoke or by the lack of oxygen in the air compared to the smoke, and she would lose consciousness and die. It seemed asphyxiation could have been marginally more pleasant if not for the burning and choking of her lungs as the smoke filled it.

More importantly, as a dead woman, she would no longer have the opportunity to finish her work. With no protege to succeed her, no one then, would complete it. She finds it unlikely that another would follow her example, given the gruesomeness of her impending death and the superficially nonsensical representations of what her work meant for humanity. The casual observer finding her research, and not being put off by her untimely end, would likely find her work to be the product of religious fundamentalism having infiltrated scientific inquiry rather than a calm and measured exploration of evidence leading to the new discoveries. But it is precisely the fervor of faith that was required for the persisting in this particular brand of scientific research. Anyone without the sufficient faith would give in at the first roadblock and never pick back up the thread again. And, as she discovered just preceding this explosion, faith was the fundamental ingredient missing from the materialistic formulations behind Absurd Energy. Without it, Absurd Energy couldn't be synthesized, even if all other ingredients were perfectly combined and heated. All that would happen without faith was explosion, death, and destruction as Lucy is finding out lying under burning bits of metal and slowly suffocating in the materialist products of her own frantic research. It has become apparent that even Lucy's faith was lacking in what was required to produce such a powerful substance.

Lucy contemplates the question—how does one have faith when all evidence points to the nullification of that in which one supposedly needs to have faith? It is ultimately a paradox. In order to create something that requires faith to create, and is otherwise impossible, one must possess an infinite imagination capable of creating new rules for the world in which they live without the help of the Absurd Energy they seek to create to help them do just that. It would be impossible to have the level of faith required for its synthesis without the immense creative ability possessed by none other than a deity. Without possessing the ability to create worlds, one could not create infinite creation. But yet, she had proved otherwise that it was, in fact, possible to create this Absurd Energy. The mathematical models proved it conclusively, regardless of what her less ambitious colleagues and mentors thought. But the only way to realize the mathematical models was to believe in the possibility of infinite creation and so make the mathematical models meaningless to begin with. A woman of science, Lucy had been unable to make the leap of faith necessary for the heroic act that was the synthesis of Absurd Energy. She had been incapable of thinking outside of the mathematical models and so, instead of reaping the rewards of her success, she instead burns to a crisp and suffocates on the products of her labor, infinitely creating the despair and misery of her failures and is subsequently buried in a closed casket.

The holes weren't dug yet, so the undertaker leaves the box on the ground next to the plot that'd been picked out and purchased, and so she lies with her embalmed body baking from the sun beating down on the black walnut exterior and filling the cushioned interior with chemical humidity. It is a hot day, and all the men sweat through their suits, and all the women fan themselves with programs from the funeral, and some wear wide-brimmed hats to keep the sun off their faces. The priest speaks some words and the cemetery employees stand under the shade of a tree a few hundred yards away and smoke cigarettes and joke quietly between themselves, quiet enough that no one mourning could hear what they are saying —or even what they are joking about necessarily—but loud enough that a faint murmur could be heard, carried over on the stagnant wind just behind the calm and practiced monologue. Some others cry. No one seems to notice the two cemetery workers standing over by the trees smoking and joking amongst themselves. It is fine that they stand off and watch; there is nowhere else for them to be, and they can't be blamed for light conversation while they wait to get to work. But the hole should have at least been dug ahead of time. There had been work to be done before the burial, and they had shirked it to stand off by the trees and smoke cigarettes and joke amongst themselves. Now people collect around the plot of land designated and purchased for the occasion and weep lightly to themselves so as to not steal the spotlight from the priest and the dark, wooden box lying heavy in the grass next to where the hole should have been.

After the priest finishes talking, he bows his head, and mutters several prayers under his breath, and the collection of people bow their heads, and listen, and say their own prayers, and there is a moment of silence, and then everyone disperses. The priest lays a hand on the top of the casket on his way by and says another quick prayer before walking to his car and driving back to his rectory. The coffin is left on the grass, and the cemetery workers walk over with their shovels and their cigarettes and get to work. One takes a last drag and flicks the butt back toward the small road that cuts around and through the hills of buried bodies before sinking his shovel into the earth. It is a hot day and, after only a few shovelfuls, both sweat from the exertion.

"I'm sorry for your loss," one says in between shovelfuls.

"Thank you."

"Are you just going to watch?" the other says.

"Mickey, don't be a dick," the first says.

"I'm just asking," the other says.

"It's ok," I say. "Do you mind if I watch?"

"Watch away."

They go back to their work in silence, the first embarrassed for the second. The digging goes quickly to start until they make it a few feet and start dragging rocks out of the hole. Struggling against the weight of stone, they continue and eventually disappear almost entirely into the hole. Another two hearses drive through the gate to the cemetery and wheel slowly around the narrow road, stopping over by where the two cemetery workers had been smoking during the service. Four more men clad in black suits step out of each car and pull two more black coffins out of the backs of them to carry over to the plot that had been designated and purchased for the purpose.

"We're done digging. Do you want to say anything else?" the first cemetery worker says.

"No, thanks."

The cemetery worker shrugs, and he and his coworker lift the casket off the ground to lower it into the hole before shoveling the excavated dirt on top, clattering rhythmically. The four men from the hearses on the road stop by the grave and set down the two additional coffins before returning to their cars and driving away. One nods in consolation as he spins on his toes and, back in their cars, they continue driving their hearses around the narrow road loop back to the gate at the entrance to the cemetery, disappearing onto the main road. When the cemetery workers finish burying one, they begin digging holes for the other two on either side. They could have at least had the hole ready ahead of time.

Finally on the edge of the city, Johanna thought again about the world she created. She longed to be in that machine, to experience the utopia she had created, to interact with the beings there. For a moment she considered turning back on the outside hope she would be found innocent, but shook her head against that impossibility and instead trudged forward.

IV

After the reverberations of profanity quieted in the room, Ed's gaze settled on Lucy, and a silence fell again, choking out the air, as all the breath was held in common by Lucy and Ed, waiting for its desperate, choking release. Lucy could see the fury rising in Ed's eyes but was still certain of his passivity. He wouldn't snap in any meaningful way, but as always, lob a snarky comment her way—one that always felt more clever to Ed than to anyone else—and use that release to vent the pressure of anger that always seemed to be pressing against his throat, pressing whatever remained into some unfillable hole at the bottom of his being. She watched his body go rigid, his hands involuntarily grip whatever was in front of them, his nostrils flare. And now, starting with a pulsing relaxation of his grip, he began to ease out of his rage— but his grip didn't loosen as expected; instead, he leaned forward in his chair, still holding the arms as if to prepare to launch himself out of it and at Lucy.

As she watched her brother coil like a snake, she wondered if she'd gone too far with her words, that she was at fault for her mother's exit, that her mother, if not justified in her obstinance, was at least justified in her departure. Her words, the last bit at least, were not meant as an attack, necessarily—Lucy had given up trying to convince her mother of anything by that point. Instead, and she would have sworn this to anyone who asked, she chalked up these most recent words to idle musings, not meant to hurt or convince. With sudden shock, she realized that even if she hadn't intended to hurt, it was clear she did, and wondered if her unintentional wounding of her mother's pride demonstrated that she was somehow evil, or if not evil, broken, or if not broken, bitter at the long history of hostility between them. She wondered to what degree latent bitterness had tainted her interactions with her mother as an adult, and to what degree she could ever hold a genuine opinion about anything her mother did or decided.

V

The bottle of translucent tequila sits tepid behind the bar in front of Sanna—chin on hands, staring through the distorted glass and into the depths of it. It refuses to reply to her slurred questions and demands, and The Bartender refuses to continue serving her, and her body refuses to support itself or straighten its spine. Her eyes are glazed, no longer their piercing green but now a milky emerald, soaking with the tequila that now is only residual in the glass by her head. At the bottom of the bottle in front of her, a small worm floats in circles in an armless backstroke, ignoring Sanna.

"They always say there's truth at the bottom of a bottle, but really there's just a stupid bug," Sanna says. "You're just a stupid bug. I'm better off talking to the glass bottle you're in. At least that will give me a reflection of myself. Stupid fucking bug."

Sanna closes her eyes and hiccups and takes the final sip from the residual tequila in the bottom of her glass. The Bartender emerges from the back, sweating from the heat in the kitchen, and takes her glass with him after filling another with ice and water for her to sip on.

"I don't want this. I don't want this water. If you're gonna serve me at all, give me more to drink. You know what I want. It's the same thing I've been ordering this whole damn time!" Sanna sighs and adjusts her weight on the barstool, nearly falling to the floor in the process, but righting herself before the stool collapses beneath her. She swallows hard against the sticky tequila saliva in her mouth and takes a deep, bleary-eyed breath.

"That's the thing, though, you stupid fucking worm. People always say there're answers at the bottom of the bottle some-times, and what they think they're saying is that the alcohol clears your head and the inhibitions in there so you act more readily or whatever the fuck. But they're really talking about talking to you. Or like, reading tea leaves or some shit. At the end of it, it's just about removing the responsibility of choice and action from your own life and coping with the unpre-dictability of things outside your control with superstition. That's all it is, and it's pathetic. It's pathetic when people recommend a drink to clear your head and it's pathetic when I come down here and drink so I don't have to think about the patients I've lost, and the patients I can't treat, and how random and pointless the whole fucking thing is. Because it *is* ulti-mately pointless, and if that's the case, there's no answer anywhere—not in the bottom of a glass, not in talking to some dead worm or inanimate object, or even talking to the barkeep of the shitty fucking dive you're in. The only place the answers exist is in your head. And those answers are made up answers that don't mean anything. You can come up with all the answers you want, but the problem is, there's no answer key to check them against. So whatever answer you come up with you have to justify yourself. But what happens when you can't justify anything anymore? Then you're fucked up a creek. Then you're shit-housed at a shitty dive bar at four o'clock on a fucking Wednesday afternoon knowing you're not going to come up with a better answer than every other time you've looked for one, but you look either way because it's the process of looking that's become necessary, not the answer at the end of it all. But that's not really satisfying either because then you're stuck in an eternal loop of desperate longing. So here's to that. Time to take a fucking drink! Barkeep! Another for me and my friend here!"

The Bartender rolls his eyes and ignores Sanna as she wobbles and tumbles from her barstool, down to the floor, into her hole, safe with her stone placed secure above her head. My hole is only just wide enough for my head to slip through, and it settles comfortably around my neck, draping down my shoulder. This is the moment I'd been building up to, and now it had come, standing up with me with my head approaching the rafters in the ceiling, a hole punched in the sheetrock to access one, and dust and chunks of gypsum and paper littered around the feet of the chair. The moment tells me it's now time, and the chair falls from under my feet while the hole tightens, and gravity takes its hold, and my internal organs leap into my throat. They have nowhere to go with the hole cinching around my windpipe and staying stuck in my voice box, choking out the involuntary sound that comes out when the rope goes taut and the rafter groans against my weight. The green has thickened outside and traces of it seep in through the cracks in the walls and make the entire place smell like rotting eggs. My feet tremble. Choking inside or choking outside, nothing else is possible now. The only choice is when and by whose hand. There is no more sense in waiting. There are no thoughts left to have, and the only ones that remain loop in my head like magnetic tape, each rotation accruing more glitches and video scratches as the magnetic filings fall out of the plastic. The only way to stop the glitches is to stop playing the tape, an impossibility in my current state. My feet struggle for purchase, trying to betray the will of what little mind remains in my skull. Thus ends the line of these pathetic, exiled kings—I give up the bloodline. It is no longer mine to have.

Across the room, on a table relegated to the corner, an old picture frame stands with a picture of a man boarding an airplane in a pilot's uniform. He stands halfway up the stairs between the tarmac and the side hatch and has turned to flash a smile at the photographer. The image comes and goes as I spin on the end of the line, a fish gasping for air through my despair. I stand on the stairs and grin, about to fly my first long-haul flight after finishing training, proudly displaying my double-stripe, having been hired as a second officer. The photograph fades out, and I welcome the final embrace of oblivion.

The Fourth Turn

i

T he Company is excited to announce the newest in our line of augmented realities available upon the basis of a yearly contract that will be negotiated at time of purchase. *In summary, this newest line of realities is nothing short of a miracle.*

The air is green outside, but there is a door and windows and walls that separate the inside from the out. The green is leaking in, but it has not yet penetrated catastrophically. Instead, I wait and watch it slowly leak in and contaminate. Instead, I watch my own entropic decay. Good Lord, why must I suffer this? What must I do to escape with my life intact? This is not possible, and now the innocent must reap the consequences sowed by the absent sinners. Now we are all sinners condemned to die for our associations. God, save me. Please. It all is too much, and I am not sure I am able to bear much more of this burden. This cross has become too heavy to continue carrying, and my feet have sunk so deep into the sand that I can no longer lift them out and continue to step forward. I cannot do anything but sink downward into despair and terror of what is to come. I cannot imagine anything other than this waiting with the green outside and myself burdened by entropy inside. Soon, there will be no more inside, and the green will have taken it all. There will be no more experience and with it, no more existence. What happens then when everything falls away to reveal the Absolute? If that is where we're headed, that is. My soul, so petrified as it is, will transcend this body to find what on the other side? When all the remaining evil falls away, when it is stripped down to the bare essence of creation, what then is left? Without the interplay between good and evil, nothing is left. Without evil, there can be no good. With only good, there is nothing, annihilated by its opposite. We haven't been good for a long time, have we?

🍾

Our finest engineers have worked tirelessly to bring you Gaiaform, the pinnacle in artificial reality simulation.

🍾

So then all will fall away without observers. What then will be left? How can anything be left without observation? And if you, the eternal observer, are no longer left—having been killed to incapacitate all evil—then already, there must be nothing left, and I am just the fading observer within a dying consciousness. How I mourn Your mortification saving us from evil but destroying in the process and leaving us with nothing at the end. There couldn't be anything at the end and therefore, nothing for the duration can really be put to use either. All it would take is to put it into an order. All I needed was some kind of story to tell, but there is no story to tell, at least not anymore. Maybe there was one once, but that story has been too heavily deconstructed. Now, only fragments fall apart in the dying light of God. Save me, please. Teach me, tell me what is happening to me, return me to those who love me. There is no me without the many others contributing to the story—alone I am an old, forgetful man unable to remember who he is. Remind me who I am, be the reason and rationality I so desperately need in this time of entropy and falling away. And if there will be no after, if there will be nothing when all else falls away, let it fall quickly and obliterate itself fully in the dirt. My suffering is too great, and I cannot bear to lie here wondering much longer. The great End is upon me, and I can neither bear to wait nor hasten its coming. There is no spirit to bear it nor rope to finish it. The green is outside, and I am inside and all of the pieces are falling apart. The green is coming to take me away, and all I want is to be reunited with my wife and my kids. But she and they are safely buried with rocks over their heads. I will not be safely buried. All I will be is an old man alone in a chair, terrified of the end and waiting for God to come back to life and permeate everything, and bring me peace.

Unlike other simulations that are populated by computed and code-based automatons that merely emulate human consciousness, the populations of Gaiaform are, in fact, autonomous beings that visitors can interact with in any way that's chosen— so long as it abides by our rules of operation.

Oh, such peace I'm sure will never come while I can see the green encroaching around me, so I should gouge out my eyes, so I no longer have to look at it. Oh, such peace I'm sure will never come while I can smell its vile odor, so I should cut off my nose. Oh, such peace I'm sure will never come while I can hear its whispers drifting in through the cracks in the door, so I should poke holes in my eardrums and mutilate shut the openings. Oh, such peace I'm sure will never come while I can taste the putrid product of a decomposing world, so I should rip my tongue straight from my throat. But oh, such peace will still not have come while I still have a mind, so I should snuff it. But I have run out of rope and spirit and even then, I'm sure, it would still prove futile. Alas, I must wait and rot here, absent from my wife and kids safely buried with stones on top of their heads.

These rules are easy to follow and ensure the optimal gameplay for everyone while maintaining the integrity of the simulation.

I

Fully coiled, Ed launched at Lucy, releasing his frustration in a single, pithy attack. "What the fuck was that?" Still unable to see her brother as in any way aggressive, Lucy let his words wash over her, fazing her in her dumbfoundedness about as much as a stiff breeze. She followed his ragged breaths with her eyes and watched his shoulders rattle at the terminus of each inhalation—now he was desperate to gather himself back up into the guarded facade he felt most comfortable being. Before he could, Lucy clicked back into the present and lashed out at him in defense, not harmed by his words, but primed for aggression by habit.

"What the fuck was what? At least I'm making a damn effort—I was hoping you'd be more than just my ride." Just as quick as he had it, he lost his footing and faltered away from his early outburst. Lucy, recovered from her reverie, leaned forward, elbows on knees, and continued her assault. "Just once in your goddamn life, it'd have been nice for you to actually have my back instead of cowering behind me. She's our mother; I would have thought you'd by now be able to have a genuine conversation with her as a grown-ass adult rather than hardly being able to even acknowledge when she's being a dick, let alone call her on it." Gaining steam, Lucy lifted off the couch, almost crouching over it, pushing Ed further into his chair. Peter ground his teeth gently and silently across the room, drawing no attention from his children. Lucy continued. "Hell, if I didn't know you, I'd think you're trying to undermine the whole reason we're here."

"That's not fair," Ed said, breathy and afraid. "I just don't think having a yelling match with her is going to change her mind any."

"How the hell am I supposed to get through to her, then? You know as well as I do that she's not going to let us in unless we push her."

"You haven't even tried—"

"Oh fuck off. Stop acting like this is the first conversation we've ever had with the woman."

Ed slouched into his chair, moping against Lucy's swift rebuttal. In response to his passivity, Lucy began to calm, twitching occasionally with the remnants of her wrath and the subconscious pride of repeated victory over her brother. She could hear the clinks of glasses and bottles in the next room where her mother had escaped, and Ed glanced over his shoulder as the sounds pulsed into the living room.

ii

Side by side they lie awaiting...Side by side they lie...
Side by side... Buried safely with stones set upon their
heads awaiting... They rip the speech from their
tongues, and the sounds from their ears, and the sights from
their eyes, and for them, all is dark, and cold, and quiet. The
cushions of their coffins support their eternal waiting and
decay, springing forth nothing but old bones and dust, awaiting
their eternal return, awaiting their resurrection, awaiting their
eternal becoming as they eternally decompose. Off they go
awaiting into the future. Their eternal view is spent gazing
upwards at the dark wooden box, illuminated by their lack of
sight, to become an infinite expanse of empty space for them to
explore. No longer are they bound by the physical dimensions
of their graves, but are now empty themselves, free to transcend
the bounds of fullness. Their eternal music rings out muffled
lullabies, now amplified by the acoustical expanse of everything
that is not and tuned to the plucked strings of their lives. Eternally, they rest comfortably in the plush upholstery supporting
their brittle bones and powdery bodies, mingling into the

tattering cloth. They await the rap tap tap on their coffin doors telling them the time is now. *Now* has come, and the time still has not come, and so they continue to await in their luxury now convinced of their solitude and now satisfied in their peace. Soon, surely, the day of coming judgment will bring to them eternal peace. Their sense of an ending moves just out of grasp with each second ticking away, never to come but only to fizzle out eternally. They await safely buried under the ground with rocks upon their heads to mark them when God finally comes to take them up from their peaceful slumber.

First and foremost, offerings must be presented from within the simulation as a form of payment for one's continued stay within the world. These offerings must be given in the form of digital currency, what we refer to as tithes, that can be generated in-game by participation in the endogenous economy, working directly for The Company, or by managing the assets and debts of the NPCs. Upon leaving the simulated world, any wealth generated in-game can be converted into over-world currency for a small conversion fee. Additionally, any over-world wealth can be converted for use in the simulation and payment plans can be set up so working for tithes in the simulation is unnecessary. We at The Company encourage you to live in the game to the full limits of your imagination and contact us with any suggestions or ideas for how you wish to play the game.

But many do not await; instead they prevent the unpreventable. Sanna fights against the irrevocable—in front of her, perfect expanses of skin stretch across bone and a host of other connective tissues, lying across exam tables. She prods the beautiful skin, and the skin recoils from her instruments. She prods again and the skin recoils again. She prods again and holds her instruments fast against the surface of the skin, and it bubbles and vibrates as if in a scream. Blisters begin to form around the periphery of the point of contact between the instruments and the skin that opens and oozes before scabbing over and disappearing as the skin repairs itself and sloughs off the scab. Blisters form and disappear, and still the skin bubbles and screams.

"It appears as though your burns are healing nicely," Sanna says. "But I'm worried about some areas that look like the beginnings of infection." She presses again, elsewhere along the surface, spurring a new bubbling of blisters and silent screams in pain. "We'll keep an eye on those spots of infection. Let me know if they get any worse—if they start itching or oozing in a way that doesn't look right—and I'll come check on them now and then. If they get any worse, I'll probably have to excise them. In the meantime, I'm going to start you on a course of antibiotics to help avoid that possibility."

Sanna prods a few more sections of the skin producing the same bubbling and screaming. Satisfied, she rolls her chair to the next spread of skin on bone on the exam table and presses her instruments against it, eliciting the same response. She holds them until blood begins to pool on the surface of otherwise flawless skin.

"It appears the fractures are fairly severe and are going to take a while to heal. But given the nature of your accident, I'd say you got out pretty lucky. The lacerations should heal faster, but make sure you don't pick at them. We want to minimize the amount of scarring. Other than that, and some physical therapy to overcome the sedentary lifestyle you'll have to live until you heal, you should recover perfectly well."

She smiles and presses the end of her instruments against

the skin one last time, leaving a handful of blisters on the surface when she removes them. Rolling on to the last stretch of skin over bone on the exam table, she again prods, resulting in blisters and audible screaming. The blisters don't heal and begin to ooze uncontrollably. She removes her instruments.

"It looks like there's nothing wrong with you, so we're going to have to discharge you. I know you came in with symptoms, but sometimes these things clear up on their own and keeping you here would be a waste of your time and money. I assure you, everything is going to be fine. Please just rest and come back if the symptoms reappear or you have any other issues you want to have looked at."

She reaches out with a gloved hand and pats reassurance on the stretch of skin, leaving a hand-shaped imprint of screaming, oozing blisters. Sanna stands from her chair and leaves these three blistering, screaming stretches of skin on their own to heal from their ailments, and goes to heal herself from the ailments that afflict her.

Johanna sat in a back storage room, papers scattered on the table in front of her, with The Company's bulletin playing over a speaker on one of the shelves in the corner. She fiddled with several of the papers—a map of logistics networks, several written briefs—and quickly scrawled writing onto another blank paper. She folded it quickly and stuffs it into an envelope before knocking a fist on the door behind her. A young man, barely old enough to grow the stubble sticking out at odd angles from his face, opened the door and took the envelope from Johanna.

"Where are we at with the surveillance unit?" Johanna asked.

"*They radioed a few minutes ago. They're coming back and will give you the full report.*"

"*Good. Let me know when they've returned.*"

Johanna returned to her work, but the young man remained in the doorway fiddling with the envelope.

"*Um... Commander?*" *Johanna turned back to the door.* "*Initial reports aren't good. Sounds like the whole city is lined up to be plugged in.*" *Johanna nodded.*

"*Yes, we expected this. They just want to escape. That's not a surprise.*"

After a moment, the young man steeled himself and nodded, closing the door on his way to deliver the envelope.

II

"Is Mom drinking?" Lucy said after a moment of listening to the cacophony of glass coming from the other room. Unsure how to answer, Ed looked back and forth between the doorway to the kitchen and his sister. She stirred on the couch, considering running to the doorway to lambaste their mother for intemperance, ultimately looking to her brother for guidance, suddenly finding herself with doubt in herself and her approach leaking in through holes in her facade she didn't know existed. After a moment, she settled back into the couch. "I didn't know she drank this early in the day."

"We don't know what she's drinking."

A cork popped in the other room, silencing all further doubt Ed had. Again, Lucy stirred, this time poised to leap up and excoriate Sanna for leaving them alone to have a shaky drink in the other room, for refusing to acknowledge the reality in which she was living, for refusing to take her daughter seriously after a lifetime of writing her off. The holes in her earthen facade opened further and kept her weighted down to the spot as doubt rushed in to fill the vacuum. "We need to talk to her," Lucy said in a harsh whisper. "She's got to see the hypocrisy in what she's saying with a bottle in her hand. If the hill she's dying on is 'taking care of Dad is an extension of her nursing career,' then this has to be a violation of her code of conduct."

Ed nodded, otherwise not responding for a moment. Watching Lucy ready herself to spring out of her seat, he took a deep breath and held out his hand to stay her. "Yes, we should try again. But—but, we need to try a softer approach."

"Ed, no. I already told you—"

"You also already drove our mother to drink at..." Ed checked his watch and looked back up at his sister. "About two in the afternoon. It seems to me that delicacy would be in our best interests here."

Lucy stood and took several steps toward the door, each one vanishing in confidence. Ed stood to follow her, passing her, and leading the two of them into the kitchen, leaving Peter alone in his chair, still staring off into space, eyes still glazing over, limbs rigid against the cushions.

iii

This new chair digs into the back of my hips, but there isn't a nurse or doctor around to help me adjust. The bones are still too broken and pasted loosely back together to move comfortably or easily. Whoever had pushed the chair out to the edge of the parking lot had since left, and whoever was coming to meet me here had not yet arrived. Casting layers up and around my arms, shoulders, and neck make it impossible to look behind me to even see if someone has come to either bring me back to wait elsewhere or else to push me further out to find whoever was coming to take me away. The air is cold, and I shiver against the ocean breezes migrating in from the coastline through the trees; the air only warms slightly from the exhaust pipes of cars and the chimneys sticking out of roofs. It isn't warmed enough to not pierce through the plaster onto my naked chest and flow into the crevices between the cast and the skin. A sign by the entrance to the parking lot advertises this property belonging to the Carney Hospital, but there are no memories of whether I had just been there and now was leaving or had come seeking treatment for some ailment. There is no way to prove that there is, in fact, a building behind me that is the hospital except for a long shadow cast over me and my chair that keeps the sun from warming me against the breeze. The only thing I know is the shadow of the hospital stretched by the setting sun onto the parking lot in front of me, the shadow of my visit, the empty expanse of lot, and my waiting. The only thing to do is stare forward and await whatever it is that will happen, whoever it is that will come, if anyone is on their way, and try to make do with the edges of the chair pushing into my back and hips in the meantime.

Johanna continued poring over her map as the speaker played in the corner. Irritated, she suddenly stood and pulled the plug out of the wall, silencing the incessant dictation of rules and regulations for gameplay. With a sigh, she reveled in the new silence for a moment and returned to her seat. She already knew what The Company was planning, and the surveillance team had consistently confirmed all of this in the lead up to release, but it still pained her to think about what they were doing with her creation—what they were doing to the lives of both the simulated and non-simulated. But the pain was necessary impetus to create a better world—she knew this too. What began as a campaign to liberate the innocent creatures she had created had become a campaign against The Company and for the people of both worlds. The attack would happen, and when the people came to realize the full extent of the grip The Company had over them, and when they realized that all they were given was enough to keep them complacent, dead automatons no different than what The Company envisioned her creation to be, they would rally their support for her. It would be a difficult struggle, but a necessary one, an inevitable one. But with the support of the people, it would be one they would win.

But behind me, inside the hospital, he, my son, my beautiful boy, the fruit of my loins, the projection of myself into post-humous life—he lies silently staring in his six-foot-by-six-foot psychiatric cell knowing nothing of the world around him except for the feeling of his bedspread and mattress. His eyes are glazed and peer ominously into the depths of his mind, a world he created for himself as rejection of the one he found himself in. Oblivious, or at least uninterested in outside stimulus, he remains locked in the fantasy he created, suffering occasionally from the terrors that his subconscious created without his knowledge. He is a well-respected philosopher of mind, the greatest in fact, learning all he did by the work of his own psychic explorations, and helping no one with his discoveries. He tried, oh how hard he tried to help, but the discoveries he found were not even suitable for saving himself. His discoveries died with him. Or at least they will die with him. Or are they dying with him? He is still kicking, but all signs indicate his life will become a waste, the scrawled note of a bored student into the margins of a history built by the random action of opposing particles. It isn't the green that takes him, but it may as well have been for all the good those posthumous years would have done for him, kept stashed away where he would be safe until he could be buried safely with a stone placed on his head to mark him for the reuptake. The doctors said it is always a problem of reuptake, that his brain was too flooded, and his body wanted no responsibility for the creation of its chemical byproducts. Maybe he is a brain chemical waiting to be taken back up into the hospital's neurons. They are just as full of themselves as anyone could have been—I sure as hell didn't have a better answer—and we all know they are talking best guesses and statistical trends that may or may not have had anything to do with his situation. It was absurd to think, given the collective experience contradicting his postulations, but it is always possible in the most minuscule of probability, that he is right in his assertions. There would be no way to know for sure, of course, but the slightest chance of it always leaves me shaking. Now, there is no more shaking nor anything left to do but wait. He does a good job waiting, and I hope to live up to his example.

The day the plug-in center opened, the line for signup stretched from the front desk all the way back to the shuttle entrance with more trying to sneak through the line from the street. Soon, even the sidewalks were crowded with a mass of fanatically desperate people looking for a pay-as-you-go vacation financed by The Company. People waited days, sending members of their party on errands for supplies and camping where they stood in line when the night came. Among these masses of hopefuls waiting, unguarded and in starry-eyed dazes, pickpockets and thieves mingled, taking what they could unnoticed. And some did not notice. And some did not care in the shadow of the gloried peace that the simulation would hold for them—as long as not so much was taken as to threaten to prevent them from reaching the front of the line. Thus a parasitical balance was found among the thieves and hopefuls creating its own economic ecosystem separate from the watchful eye of The Company.

III

In the kitchen, Sanna sat at the table with a bottle of gin, a bottle of soda water (both left open), and a glass half-full with the sparkling mixture. She threw back what was left in her glass and replenished one part gin to three parts soda, narrowly avoiding spilling over the rim, clanking the bottles around with haste. After a sip, she looked up to find her children standing in the doorway, watching her in silence. "Have you come to harass me further?" Sanna said. "Your old mother, wanting nothing more than a nice visit with her children?" Before Lucy could speak, Ed took a step forward and cut her off.

"No, Mom. I just didn't know you were much of a drinker."

"Eddy, my sweet boy. Can I make you a drink?" The gin had begun trickling over her eyes and soothing her battered ego, starting her quickly on the path toward bloodshot fatigue. Leaving Lucy in the doorway, Ed sat across from his mother with his elbows on the table. Sanna saw through his concern and smiled back at him before standing and taking a glass from the shelf. "Lucy? One for you as well?" Lucy shook her head, restraining herself from speech out of fear of losing control. Sanna ignored her response and set two more glasses on the table, filling them at the same proportion as hers, only stopping much shorter of the rims. "I don't really need a drink," Ed said. "But thank you." Sanna pushed his drink toward him and held Lucy's up outstretched in her direction. Slowly, Lucy moved closer and sat between her mother and brother, cupping her drink in front of her. After a moment, Ed spoke again. "Mom, I promise you we're not coming here to attack you. We're genuinely concerned for you and Dad and want to make sure you're both getting the care you need." Sanna pretended not to hear her son and instead, stared into her drink as if a crystal ball.

"Your father introduced me to drinking, you know. After he was off duty one night, he picked me up and we drove up to St. Louis. He wanted to take me to get a drink and claimed that this one lounge—I can't for the life of me remember the name of it—was the only place in the city to get a proper drink. He had a disdain for what he called 'the vodka-cranberry swill on every corner.'" Sanna took a sip of her drink and swirled it around, not taking her eyes off the vortex of ice and bubbles. "I wasn't brave enough for any of the dark liquors, so I settled on gin, since it was the closest thing I could get to vodka without offending him." Sanna laughed to herself, fully locked into the memory. Lucy took a small sip and kept the glass pressed against her lips, flicking her eyes in Ed's direction now and then. He sat still, waiting patiently for the end of the story so he could steer his mother back to the topic at hand. "I can't remember what the drink was called, but it was gin; it was both flowery and citrusy, it had a touch of bubbles, and was the best drink I'd ever had at the time and is still up there even now." Sanna held up her glass. "This is a pathetic reproduction, but it'll have to do for now." She drained her glass with precision and set to refill.

"Mom," Ed said. "Why don't you slow down a little bit? We have all afternoon." Sanna ignored him and refilled her drink, taking a slow sip while locking in eye contact with her son. With a sigh, Ed took his glass and took a small sip, mirroring her. They both set them down, a little too hard in front of them.

"There you go," Sanna said. "It's a nice afternoon spritzer, isn't it?"

"It's fine, thanks."

"Lucy, how are you enjoying yours?" Lucy nodded, taking another sip to keep herself from speaking. Happy that she and her children could now enjoy a casual afternoon together with a light drink in hand, she smiled at each of them in turn. "It's so nice that you both are here. It gets lonely sometimes up here. Please don't take that as a guilt trip—your father and I love the solitude—we just wish you'd visit more, but we understand that you're busy. I'm glad you're here now."

"It's nice to be here too," Ed said. He took another sip of his drink and continued. "Can I ask you a question, and can you give me a straight answer?" Sanna nodded, mid-sip, bobbing up and down with her drink as if floating in it. "I mean this as delicately as I can. Why are you afraid of having Dad in a nursing home?" Sanna choked on her drink before setting it down in front of her, wiping her mouth, and replacing the distant smile on her face. Lucy took a quick swig of her own drink, glancing between her mother and brother. Sanna chuckled quietly to herself.

"That reminds me of one time—oh, I think it was in '78 maybe? Maybe it was later than that. It was shortly before we moved to New Hampshire." Sanna waved her away with her hand. "Anyway, you know how your father is about heights. I wanted to take him up the water tower on Bissell Street—"

"Mom, you said you'd give me a straight answer."

"Honey, please don't interrupt me. It's quite rude." Ed sighed and gave in. Lucy, seeing the conversation moving in circles around her mother's deflection, finished her drink and slammed it against the table.

"Enough, Mom. Fucking enough." The room went silent. Sanna and Ed both looked at Lucy in horror while Lucy waited for her mother to lash out again at her.

iv

Lucy doesn't die from the explosion of machines and radioactive chemicals poisoning unventilated spaces and roasting the biological matter inside. She dies waiting and watching her faith in what she otherwise knows is impossible slowly dwindle and disappear as her machines and equations keep plugging along, not needing external input to continue their trajectory randomly through space. She does a good job waiting, too. She does a good job consuming the energy provided to her and putting it toward something of intrigue, despite that intrigue ultimately being a wasted enterprise. By her death, her duty is done—she firmly contributes, perhaps more than others, to furthering the motion of entropy on into the dark ahead. She creates machines that serve no purpose but to disseminate energy out into unusable states that could continue to be stored in the base layer of existence, equally serving no larger purpose. She creates her machines in her own image, a mindless consumer producing nothing of value.

Compounding the wait, the induction process was hampered by technical bugs owing to the complexity of creating so many avatars from scratch and correctly mapping those digital minds to their physical complements. Many errors were encountered, and only most of them were able to be resolved.

She spends her days watching the gears turn and feeding in more and more, having not even bothered building an output channel for whatever products she is attempting to make. She knows what she is doing—she is a master of creating contraptions whose sole purpose is to consume, contraptions in her own image, eternally consuming on the promise of some mystical realization of worth and value, knowing full well that ultimate value is based upon a myth she had created from the wallows of despair in order to continue on in her true task: the great march toward darkness. She completes her mission with valor and ingenuity so that she can finally rest in peace buried safely under the ground with a stone placed on her head to mark the resting place of a true hero. Continuing on when no one else saw the point, she reaps all that she deserves.

IV

After a moment of waiting through the startled silence in the room, Lucy spoke again. "For fuck's sake, Mom. You gotta talk to us. We're your children, and as much as you don't seem to want us to, or we may not really want to, we care about you and Dad and are worried about everything happening." Sanna's hand trembled, and she gripped her glass to steady it, taking the opportunity to bring it to her mouth for another sip. Lucy waited, and Ed held his breath in shock, completely ruptured from any control he may have had in this most recent iteration of their conversation. Without warning, Sanna let out a sob, nearly choking on her drink in the process, and collapsed onto her elbow on the table, spilling some of her drink as she fell. Lucy glanced over to her brother and back to her mother, but it was not a ruse; Sanna truly had broken. And this sob was the first bubble to rise to the surface after several years of seething pain watching Peter deteriorate and after the sudden heat of the afternoon. She sucked ragged breath, contemplating another sip of her drink to try and stave off her roiling emotions below. But the steam had built up and blown cracks in the shell she had built up around herself. No longer would her faculty for misdirection succeed; instead, attempts at changing the subject would be clumsy and senile, encouraging her children worryingly close to thinking her mind was beginning to go as was her husband's.

But still, she had nothing to say, nothing to contribute to her worried children trying desperately to help her, bless them. And they, for their part, seemed not to expect their latest attempt to succeed in breaking through to the core of her thoughts and feelings, and now they were equally hushed. Instead of a breakthrough, open sharing between three equally concerned parties, Lucy stared at Sanna in shock—having never succeeded in breaking through her mother's defenses in her life; Ed began sipping his drink with greater speed—now sensing another, even more caustic explosion on the horizon, what with the added heat of emotional sincerity; and Sanna continued to sob, gripping her drink now as if holding on to a ship in rocking waters. Sanna craved another quick belt of the drink before her, or another jigger thrown into her glass from the bottle to reinforce her spirits, but was unable to move, unable to save herself from this collapse, unable to stop the process of her outer shell fragmenting and falling into the deeps like cliffs suddenly giving way to eons of erosion. All she could feel was the splashing and crushing of stone, and it made her feel ill.

V

John Doe lies in his bed with his eyes closed and the monitors hooked up to his body beeping in a slow, irregular polyrhythm. He is motionless and the air is equally still except for the jitter of particles on the sound waves emanated from the speaker cones hidden within the machines and the slight breeze coming from the poorly installed windows on the wall parallel to his bed. No one observes as his breath inflates and deflates within his chest, adding to the gentle calamity of the air currents in the room. One of the monitors rescinds its contribution to the erratic rhythms coming out of the choir or machines, and a small amount of bile drifts up into the feeding tube traced through his nasopharyngeal cavity. The previous beep-ba-beep-ba-be-beep-ba-ba-ba simplifies into a steady beep-ba-ba-beep-ba-ba-beep, the monitor declining its continued part in the choir responsible for the shifting cadence. The bile continues to flow the wrong way through the feeding tube, and the now steady rhythm increases its tempo to match the speeding biological functions within John Doe's body. The tempo reaches a peak and John Doe's body begins to convulse in time to the frenetic dance that had begun in his observer-less room. His convulsions lessen, and the beat slows, and his breath becomes shallow and sporadic. He rests more comfortably in the regained stillness of the room as his vitals continue to slow until there is nothing but a single sinusoidal sound piercing the prior rhythms and the smooth draft from the window resting comfortably on the continuous cry from the monitors. Don't worry. The doctors and nurses are alerted. Don't worry. There's nothing they can do.

In spite of the consistent errors—and the resulting rumors of individuals being trapped in the simulation, or removed without their mental faculties, or removed with the mind and personality of someone else—most people in line did not shy away at the opportunity to experience this novelty. The promise of freedom and ease was too strong of a lure, especially among those relegated to sleeping on the sidewalks as they waited. These truly got to experience the city for what it had become since the universal transit system had been fully implemented and the underside of the neon landscape was left to rot.

V

"Mom," Lucy said. On her face, she wore her eyes pinched into her cheeks, her lips gently parted, the back of her jaw pressed against her teeth to brace herself. "I'm sorry. But please talk to us. Please—"

"Stop it," Sanna said, more abrupt than she realized. "Just... stop." Gentler, how she intended it to be. Her sobbing held steady, jostling her voice as she spoke, and finally, she found the strength to bring her drink to her mouth and numb the battering waters. "I'm trying, I'm really trying, just... give me a moment." Lucy leaned back in her chair, cradling her drink in her lap, staring down at the table, seemingly unable to look at the mother she had finally succeeding in fracturing. Taking the bottle from the center of the table, Ed poured a couple fingers into his glass, opting to drink it without the bubbles. Again, no one spoke, and Sanna's broken breaths were the only noise inside the room. Even Peter, separated by the wall, had become totally still and silent. Outside, winter birds burbled from their branches, disrupted from their migratory patterns by well-wishing suburbanites; wind licked along the bones of the house, causing them to creak; the occasional car rode by, contributing intermittent punctuation to the idyllic soundscape and then fading out over a hill. But none of this could be heard in Peter and Sanna Hastings' kitchen; it even sounded as if the clock on the wall stopped clicking in time, though the time still passed in its mushy stop-start as each one's awareness in the room shifted around in discomfort. Sanna took another quick swig of her drink and sighed heavily against her unstable emotions, unable to put off speaking any longer. "I have to be the one to do it. I know that's insane, but I have to. I can't push him off onto someone else. He's my responsibility."

"Dad is?" Ed said.

"I have to take care of him. I promised I would, and I can't break that."

"That doesn't mean you can't have help."

Sanna shook her head and swallowed more of her drink with such force that she choked again for a moment before regaining her voice. "No, you don't understand. He's my responsibility, and that responsibility is continuous. And if I break that continuity, if you or your sister break that continuity, then what's left?" Sanna looked between her children, tears beginning to form in her eyes, shaking against the force of her inner roiling. "If he leaves here, it's the first step toward death. That doesn't make any sense." She folded over onto herself, onto her hands, onto the table, covering her drink. "If I'm not the one taking care of him... I've lost him." Sanna's gin lost its foothold against her pain, and the pain shot out of her, dropping like rain into her glass. "I can't watch him die before his time."

"It's ok," Ed said. "I understand. Promise." He reached out across the table and took her hands from her face, exposing rivulets dampening channels in her papery skin. Lucy drank faster now, finishing her drink, and setting it on the table in front of her. She stood and leaned over the sink, staring at the finches leaping from branch to branch, rippling in the breeze, finding seed dispensed to the ground from an old feeder.

"I know I can't take care of him forever." Sanna's voice escaped her throat in a quick spurt of air, her words unable to have been spoken except in haste. "I know neither he nor I are young, and I know there's nothing I can do about any of it. But it's just too soon. Even in our seventies. Even having lived good lives. I'm just not ready to let him go yet."

From the sink, Lucy turned and spoke in a low voice. "Mom, I'm sorry. I thought I wanted— I mean, I didn't..." Lucy turned back to the window, ragged and tied to her mother's pain, almost miraculously, by a thread she didn't know existed. "I'm just sorry for pushing." Ed looked up at his sister and back to his mother. Silence again covered the room, except for the soft, but erratic, rhythm of Sanna's breath.

vi

Sanna leans on her folded wrists on the wooden rail on the edge of the bar and stares at the small puddle of tequila in the bottom of her shot glass. The tequila worm bathes and luxuriates in it as the nearly empty bottle sits further back next to the glass. The bar is empty and The Bartender is nowhere to be found. It is dark enough to be impossible to tell if the lights are on, but bright enough that it is impossible to conclude they are unlit. There seems to be a lightness to every object in the room despite no apparent source of that light. Sanna listens intently to the worm speaking to her in riddles.

"You are a wise doctor of the body, but you are too filled to be taught anything of substance, for substance no longer can enter. But if you must be taught, then you should be the first to speak. I have nothing to say that can be taught."

"I want wisdom, that I should be able to know what you know and understand what you understand. I'm sure I have nothing to teach you."

"I am sure you do not seek wisdom. This is not the place for wisdom. You come seeking answers to very specific questions that you confuse with wisdom and want me to answer. Quickly, then. Get on with it."

"What is the point?"

"The point is to ask the question."

"I did ask the question."

"Then you know the point."

"But you haven't answered my question."

"If I haven't answered your question, then that means you didn't ask one."

"What is the point?"

"That there isn't an answer."

"So my despair is justified?"

"Any emotion you feel is justified. What you believe to be true is what exists."

"Then I believe I am sober."

As the last word leaves her lips, the worm, and the glass, and the bottle disappear, and the bar is suddenly filled with patrons crowding around and ordering more drinks than The Bartender can possibly make. Sanna collapses under the weight of a crippling hangover and opens her eyes again alone in the twilit bar, curled on the floor. She stands and finds the worm, and the glass, and the bottle back where they had started.

"What you're saying is there is nothing beyond what I imagine. Nothing is real."

"Then why are you afraid?"

"Because I don't understand."

"Where does that fear come from?"

"I don't know."

"All you have to do to conquer your demons is to ask."

"I still don't understand."

"It's last call."

Sanna pops her head up to see The Bartender staring at her from the other side. "I'm sorry. What did you say?"

"It's last call." Sanna stares at him for a moment, and he starts pouring a glass of water for her. "Are you ok? You've been mumbling to yourself and staring at the empty shot glass in front of you for the last few minutes."

"Was I?"

The Bartender nods and sets the glass in front of her. "I'll call you a cab."

Sanna nods, more to herself than to The Bartender, and continues to stare at the empty shot glass on the bar in front of her. Her eyes begin to tear and she collapses into her hands to weep.

Those whose minds were left in the simulation—The Company maintained this was only the case for one or two users, and they were working around the clock to resolve the issue—and those who were extracted without the entirety of their minds—similarly, The Company maintained this only happened to a few, and only those who did not follow gameplay rules—continued to exist only as wisps both inside and outside the simulation. Inside, they existed as fragments of code causing bugs and constant headaches to the software support team in charge of the back-end. Outside, they remained ghosts, buried but not dead, extant, but no longer alive.

In his own way, Charlie suffered the same, bitter agony, stumbling his heap of yellowed skin through the halls, dragging a rolling IV stand behind him, dressed in a robe that had been washed too many times, and he was unshowered and trembling. There are no nurses at their station or with the patients and no doctors in the ward. Charlie walks in circles by the patient rooms, some occupied, some not, in an endless canter of withdrawal. His eyes sink into his face, and he carries on mumbling in Sisyphean circles.

"The tequila worm in its natural habitat exhibits habitual lethargy owed likely to the alcoholic state of its environment. Similar to the koala, it spends much of its time digesting and metabolizing the narcotic chemicals present in its largely inedible and insubstantial food sources. However, unlike the koala, the tequila worm's food sources give it god-like wisdom. It only requires a person to take a few sips from the tequila worm's abode in order to begin to feel the transcendent effects. Mystics seeking true transcendence, however, habitually consume vast quantities of the tequila worm's pickling substance, claiming upon their return to sobriety to have had conversations with the tequila worm, having seen the face of God, and having come to an understanding of the purpose of life. Scientific studies have not found substantial evidence to prove these claims, but many mystical societies still ritually practice the consumption of the tequila worm's bath in the attempt to come to a higher level of consciousness."

Charlie pauses outside the room John Doe died in. His body is covered with a sheet, but the coroners haven't yet retrieved the remaining body. Charlie steps into the room and crosses himself, muttering a few words into the room as if a different voice has possessed him. "It's now too late; you won't find me. I have had to escape my persecutors and have been captured anyway. But there will be someone waiting for you when you arrive." He crosses himself again, and the voice seems to have left him alone and confused at the threshold of the room. He recognizes something has happened—something mystical—and begins searching cabinets and cupboards. Not finding what he's looking for, he hobbles back to his own room, digs through a bag in the corner, and removes a sealed bottle of tequila with a small, pickled worm suspended toward the bottom. He makes a feeble attempt to hide the bottle in the folds of his hospital gown and, careful to avoid discovery, returns to John Doe's room.

Kneeling painfully to the ground by the edge of John Doe's bed, Charlie cracks the bottle seal and takes a hefty swig, wincing and clutching himself after he sets the bottle down. After he recovers, he closes his eyes and begins a monotone chant.

"Oh pickled worm, knower of the space between consciousness and unconsciousness, keeper of the liminal wisdom, guide me toward you so I may too embody the divine essence."

Another large swig, nearly a quarter of the bottle now gone. After recovering from the pain of pouring alcohol into his distended body, he continues.

"Oh heavenly spirits, fill me with your clarifying ethers, your purifying fumes, your burning rage, for I have closed my eyes to the true understanding, and I ask that you open them to your burning presence."

A third swig, a third of the bottle gone, a third, nearly paralyzing, tremor of agony. He chokes out a third chant.

"In full knowledge of what I do, I give myself over to the darkness. I give myself over to emptiness. I give myself over to faith in the light inside the blackout. Oh, Tequila Worm, guide me from your material home to your heavenly abode. I consume your waters to fill myself so that you may empty me into your wisdom."

Charlie takes a deep breath and places a hand on John Doe's arm through the sheet. Slowly, he releases his breath and resettles himself on the ground, wincing as he moves. In his other hand, he holds the bottle, hesitating for a moment before the final swig. He looks up at the bed.

"Here's to you, the only person I've met not to need the ritual to see the wisdom." And with that final utterance, Charlie raises the bottle to his lips and takes all but the last inch of liquid into his body, just enough for the worm to continue floating in the bottle. He slams the bottle down when he's done, nearly shattering the bottom, coughing and sputtering in ascetic pain, gasping against his body's rejection of the fluid and the vapors settling in his lungs and choking him. Tremors ripple through him, and slowly he recovers, breathing slow, settling into a peaceful smile. His eyes are already distant.

Several minutes later, the coroner's assistant finds Charlie on his back on the tile with a peaceful smile on his face, the tequila worm still sitting in its bottle-shrine next to him, itself also looking as if it's smiling. The assistant checks his pulse and runs back to the door.

"We need a stomach pump in here STAT!"

Charlie is not dead, but he will not remember the mysterious wisdom that powers his smile.

On the fifth day after the launch, Johanna's resistance group attacked an off-site system processing server in an attempt to cut off some processing power from the main simulation servers and produce glitches. The attack was unexpected and succeeded, downing the system and causing glitches in the rendering and internal logistics that initial reports claimed logged nearly ten thousand users off. The outage lasted twenty-four hours and no casualties were reported. The opening salvo had been fired and war between Johanna's insurgents and The Company had officially begun.

VI

"What do we have to do to take him?" Sanna said with a sigh. Lucy turned again.

"Really?" Lucy said. Ed shot her a glance and turned back to Sanna.

"Well, Lucy's called already and set everything up," Ed said. "All we have to do is drive him over." Sanna laughed, half-choking on her tears, unsurprised that Lucy had set everything up already. She laughed at her blindness, thinking that she would be able to out-maneuver her children and finding out Lucy had out-maneuvered her, proud of her daughter's cunning, sorry for the collateral damage of emotional pain. "Are you ok?"

"Yes, I'm fine," Sanna said. "I'm fine." She regained control over herself and brushed a tear from her eye. "Goddamn, I'm not ready for this." Her face began to crumple again, but she held out against the newest wave.

"I know. None of us are," Ed said.

Sanna nodded and stood. "Well, I guess I should pack his

211

things." She walked to the doorway and stopped. "You'll come too, right?"

"We'll drive you," Lucy said. Sanna nodded again and turned back into the doorway, pausing for a moment to see her husband in his chair, really seeing him through the decaying husk of dementia. The light at the center was still lit, but it was flickering and running out of wick. After letting a raggedy breath out, she went to the bedroom to collect some clothes and decoration for his new room at the nursing home. Unsure what to bring, she packed light in a small duffel bag taken from under the bed, intending to return another time with more for him.

vi

The low ceiling and tight walls create the darkened space, keeping out all saving lights and holding fast the possibility of salvation. This is the end, and that end is enforced by the pitter patter of shovelfuls raining on the outside of the low ceiling. Men and women clad in black stand around the opening into the earth, and the cassocked old man reads from his holy book, and commits me to the earth, and prays for my soul, and leaves me to wait with the others. They've been waiting a long time, and I'm not under the illusion that I'm a special case. They advise me to settle in for a long wait and suggest that I consider sleeping. The ones who've been here the longest have been asleep since before many of the others have arrived, and it had always seemed to be the best option. The difficulty is the claustrophobia and the urge to move. But if one can overcome it, it seems that sleeping is the best way to wait. It seems that sleeping through eternity is too easy of a way out, and I remember some passage read long ago by the cassocked man about keeping awake until it was time to go. It seems that remaining alert was the proper way to pass the time, even if the time was spent in agonizing slowness.

This isn't right. I am not about to be so lucky as to pass the time with others all waiting for the same thing, the same end, the same coming that would elevate us and resurrect when all was finished and done with. There would be no long black night to suffer through, and if there would be, it would have to be suffered alone, just like it had been suffered so long, so far. The green has arrived, and there is no longer any use for this solipsism.

The world now only extends to the edges of these four walls, and the green has broken through to take me beyond the confines of this room, beyond this chair, beyond the pictures and broken memories. I'm not ready, oh God, I'm not ready, yet. The pieces still haven't been picked up and sorted and put back together into an order that I'm happy with. With just a little more time, I could finish the puzzle, and then I would happily be taken away, satisfied with my work, satisfied with the reconstitution of my stories and my life. Not yet, please not yet. Tell it to wait just a little longer so I have just a little more time to finish. Surely you can find Sanna and the kids and bring them with you so we can all be taken up together. That will be all the time I need. They won't be hard to find, buried as they are safely under the ground with stones on their heads. We put the stones there specifically for this purpose, so they'd be easily found when the time came for us all to move on. If it really is time to go, at least let them come along. Of course, there is not enough time to summon them, and I know that. The green is filling the room and everything inside of it. One last glance at the few memories I've put in order—

L ight broke through the darkness, punctuating the green, replacing the green, illuminating the four walls in which Peter lay. Beneath him, a metal table wrapped and secured him with leather straps, monitors hooked to his body, and wires and tubes ran from his skin over and into an array of computers against a far wall. He opened his eyes, younger now, no longer gray, muscles and skin taught over strong bones. He lay still for a moment, unable to parse where he was, unable to remember what had happened or how he had arrived. He stretched and tried to move and became aware of the straps, and monitors, and tubes, and believed himself to be in some kind of hospital. Struggling against the straps, he managed to free himself—they were brittle and old—and he sat up, pulling wires and tubes from his body as he rose. His table sat in the middle of a dark room, surrounded by computer systems and monitors. Dust settled in the keys and crevices, on top of sheets laid across tables, long abandoned and left to sit in eternal stasis; Peter had been abandoned here. He looked for Sanna, for Lucy, for Ed, but saw only cold concrete, dusty metal, defunct computers reflecting their opposing walls and nothing else.

Peter stood, stumbling over his wooden, sleeping legs, and collapsed to his knees in front of the nearest computer array. Clawing his hands over its surface and sending clouds of dust up into the air, he searched for a power button of some kind. When he found it, pressed it, and waited, the computer remained silent. He searched for another button, pressed it, the same. And another, and another, and another. The room kept silent except for the sounds of his shuffling hands, hyperventilations, whimpering desperation. He sneezed, sending the floating dust away in eddies, and it echoed, longer than made sense for the size of the room. Standing again on his unsteady legs, he hobbled around the room, using the wall to support him, and found a small doorway hidden behind a cluster of machines. Peering inside, he saw darkness running down a narrow hallway ending in an abyss containing obsidian reflections. A single step at a time, he made his way into the darkness, drawn forward by the combination of waning disorientation and a terror he desperately tried to keep at bay. One step at a time, he came closer and closer to the reflections at the end of the hallway, staring at him like insect eyes. The end of the hallway lightened and opened into a small room; the little light available came from a series of tiny, white LED lights accompanied by the low whirring of a fan, hidden somewhere in the room. Getting closer, the insect eyes were screens, and this room too was filled with computer machinery.

He collapsed in front of one of the monitors—dark, dormant, and reflecting his panicked face—and ran his hands along its surfaces, sending even more dust up into the air. Finding a slight depression in the back corner of the screen, he pressed and a blinding light illuminated the room, sending him cowering backwards toward the hallway. The screen faded in from its piercing white into a gray screen with an unintelligible logo over the gray in a sickening green. He cowered again from the color, but couldn't place why—it felt to him as if his mind had been emptied, with only the unconscious filaments of incomplete memories hanging at the edges like half-vacuumed cobwebs floating in an imperceptible breeze. He tried to grab onto one or another of these, follow the thread back to the complete memory, but they broke in his hands and fell into dust. Despite the emptiness, there was one thought pressing outward from the basic architecture of his mind—unavoidable, though he had done his best thus far to avoid it. He was dead. He had to be. Despite the dim and disappearing memories of some prior experience of having woken up in this laboratory, it made sense to him that they would disappear in the afterlife. No heaven could exist, pure and good and filled with peace, with the baggage from one's past life weighing on their every blissful moment. But just as likely, he could conceive of a Hell in which the tormented soul yearned to remember the loves and wonderments from its life and yet could only grasp them as Tantalus did. Clearer and clearer, as the fogginess vanished, he knew with all his heart that he was dead. And he was in Hell.

He fell face-first onto the concrete floor, and he wept, yearning for some certainty to pierce through his fear and confusion, to reassure him that someone was there guiding him through whatever terror he had walked into. With a breath, he rose again, curious despite his fear of what information the computer contained. Hitting a key on the keyboard below the monitor, he saw that the green and gray screen disappeared and revealed a document to him—a report of some kind. Scanning through, he stopped on a snippet that stood out to him:

The execution of the insurgent leader marked a brief peace as her followers fell apart and turned onto one another. This was hailed as a world-changing victory for the brilliance of the Board of Directors. But what was not foreseen, was that the followers would then rally, approximately two months following, upon rumor of the discovery of a book written as direction and unification for the movement. The strikes began shortly after as public opinion turned on The Company, almost certainly due to a combination of agitation from the followers and the long-standing instability of the simulation due to repeated attacks on The Company's infrastructure. As a result, the supply chain became dangerously precarious—it was clear to all governing bodies that the citizens had collectively decided to starve themselves in protest... of what? Of the execution they had previously supported? It was unclear what exactly they were protesting, as if a sudden suicidal hysteria had descended upon the population. The effect this had is that Parliament lost faith in the Board of Directors and attempted to seize control back. This failed, largely due to the disorder caused by the strikes, and Polatinus—the ascendant Chair of the Board after his predecessor's death—used this as pretext to label Parliamentarians as members of the insurrection and order them killed. All who didn't flee to exile were killed, and Polatinus used this campaign of terror to consolidate power under his title. Thus began The Mad Years with Polatinus sending his Investigators to suspected followers, torturing those taken into custody, and killing those who confessed.

Peter stopped reading, realizing he had stopped breathing, now even more certain he had awoken in Hell. All there appeared to be in whatever world he was in was these two rooms—one with broken machinery, the other with reports of mass political upheaval and totalitarian terror in whatever existed outside of these rooms. All there appeared to be in his mind was void, empty space, cleaned out when he awoke, as if anything before this reality had been a dream that vanished in the twilight of his rising. Leaning back against the wall, he thought, hard as he could, to remember something—anything—from whatever time existed before he was brought to this place. A rope appeared around his throat, and he gasped, grabbing at it, only to find nothing. He had hung himself? He thought again, pushing past the choking sensation, finding tears dripping down his cheeks, and ethereal darkness obscuring any other detail in the room. *Please, God, I don't want to die. But if I have to, at least let me go to Heaven.*

The voice rang out from nowhere in the dark expanse in his head. Why had he hung himself if he didn't want to die? Is that why he had arrived in Hell? For rejecting his life and committing suicide? In a burst of certainty, he remembered he was sitting in a chair, the most recent memory he had. He sat with it for a while until he was sure—a chair, an unmoving gaze forward at a wall, a photograph of a pilot ascending into the cockpit with a smile on his face. It wasn't clear how this related to the hanging, but he was sure this was the last memory he had from whatever had happened before this. In a flash, another memory—he was in a chair, sipping a drink, talking to another man, also sipping a drink. The man was in the hospital; why was he drinking? They were at a bar, and both of them were old and tired. Peter was unconscious in a bed, watching himself lie under the sheets with the man sitting next to him, patting his leg with one hand, and sipping from a bottle with another, the man's skin a sickly shade of yellow. *Find me in the oblivion,* he'd said. Was this the oblivion the man spoke of?

Now settled by the regaining of some of his memories, and bolstered by the swinging of balance from unbridled fear toward increasing curiosity, he returned to the computer and started scanning through the document again. He scrolled through to the end and picked up the last paragraph:

It is unclear how many have died in the last couple years, either by Polatinus's hand or by the natural cataclysms that have rocked the world, but from information on the last census before The Company fell to provincial rule, the total population can't be greater than just below one million souls left alive. That information is four months old, and so the true number is likely significantly less than that. Optimistically, a quarter million souls are left alive, scattered among small municipalities and isolated villages, kept separate from the vapors rising from the oceans by mountain barricades. With luck they will be able to last until this tragedy has ended. It strikes this recorder of the history that it is a shame that Johanna was executed for her attempted rebellion, it is a shame her followers too did not succeed, and even more of a shame that she was right in all of it that The Company was leading us inexorably to our present doom. We were arrogant. Many of us were complacent in our semi-medicated misery and lacked the imagination to conceive of a new world. We have now been punished by whatever God is watching above us. I hope and pray the final judgment is yet to come and that we will be able to rebuild in the meantime.

Peter stood in front of the monitor, shaken by the last sentence written on the screen. He took a breath and turned back to the room he awoke in, starting the trek through the hallway, now unwilling to read any more detail about the end of this world. Halfway down the hallway, he stopped short, a tingling along his neck alerting him to some presence. Through the dark, a cloaked figure rested against the wall past the opening of the hallway, hunched over.

Peter kept still in the hallway, unsure where this figure came from, not having found any other doors in either room. The figure hardly moved, even to breathe, and for a moment, Peter thought they were dead. He crept closer, careful not to make a sound, fearful of rousing the dead. Startling Peter still, the figure shuffled their feet and coughed, then wiped the spittle from their face.

"You don't have to be afraid of me," the figure said. Peter didn't move, instead watching the figure get more comfortable on the ground and look up at him. Their face was obscured by the hood, but a beard hung through the opening, and his eyes drooped from his face under the weight of tragedy. Peter was sure this man had lived through everything he'd just read about on the computer. "Come, please sit with me. It's been lonely here for quite some time." Slowly, Peter stepped toward the man, animal instincts keeping him alert and ready to defend himself against attack.

"Where did you come from," Peter said.

"The door—they're hard to see unless you know where they are. When The Company built this place, they went for sleek. The doors are built to blend in with the walls." Peter stopped at the edge of the hallway and stared at the man on the floor. Following the line of the walls around the room, he found the door, only showing itself by a nearly imperceptible crack where it opened. "You found the computer. I was hoping you would. You read the report, I trust?"

"Some of it—is it true?"

"As true as I remember."

"You wrote it?"

"I wrote it."

Peter took a few more steps into the room and sat on the metal table he awoke on, never turning his back to the man. He glanced behind him, measuring the distance to the door in case he needed to escape. The man shuffled his hood back, revealing aging skin covered in deformities and growths, obscuring the intensity of his ice-blue eyes, burning forth and displaying this man's vitality beneath his weathered body. Peter relaxed as he considered himself to be the more spry and able-bodied man in the room.

"Where are we?"

"This is where The Company stored Johanna's simulation after she tried to steal it back from them."

"What?"

"Sorry, I know that doesn't make sense."

"I'm dead. Right? And you as well, I guess? Or are you some kind of ferryman or something?"

The man laughed, choking a little on the bursts of air. "I'm not a ferryman, or guide, or anything like that. I'm just as mortal as you are and just as alive. I'm merely here to keep watch and wait."

"Wait for who?"

"For you I think."

Peter recoiled again. "What? Wait for me? Why? What the hell is going on?" Peter's body went rigid; he was frustrated and flailing between half-understanding and complete confusion.

"Calm yourself. I know you're confused. I'm sure you're quite disoriented. You have awoken into a new world from the one you were created in, and this world has fallen apart, as you can read in the report." The man gestured down the hallway to the computer. "Johanna foretold about you, that you would come from the ashes of the world and rid the world from the clutches of The Company. It seems you have an easier job ahead of you than we thought." Peter stood from the metal table and paced around the room, from computer to computer.

"These computers are the simulation then? Or contain it, at least."

"Correct."

A sudden horror arose in Peter, draining the color from his face and throwing bile up into his throat. He stared at the man on the floor. "So I'm..."

"You have it. Say it."

"I came from the simulation? How?"

"It was a luxury resort. Many were still in it when the collapse happened and their minds corrupted. The bodies stayed alive, and you emerged in one when you died in the simulation. I've been watching it for some time now. Really quite fascinating, and brilliant on Johanna's part, assuming it was done intentionally. You had dementia at the end as a result of the corruption of the system, and that was the way in and out." Peter looked down at his hands, and then at his reflection in one of the dead monitors. He recoiled against his young face and turned back to the man.

"Is that why I can't remember anything?"

"I'm not sure, but most likely. Since you were born in the simulation, your mind never had a physical structure containing it before now. Between the dementia and potential incompatibility between the digital and organic memory capabilities, it's possible not everything could make the transition over." The man grimaced as he stood, sliding up the wall for balance and letting the cloak fall draped along his shoulders. The hood fell completely from his head. His face was grotesque, framed by wiry gray hair shooting out in all directions, meeting and combining with a beard fraying out from his chin. In his full image, Peter was stilled, the age and wisdom of the man exuding from every pore and blemish. "Listen to me, though, as I don't have time. The Company has fallen, many have died, and the air outside this room is toxic to breathe for too much time. Immediately fatal in some places and by the oceans where the toxic gasses originated. The people of the world are scattered. I have spent the last couple years studying the writings and prison letters Johanna left for us and filling in the gaps in the history. I believe you are who she foretold would come, and so the responsibility falls on you, one way or anoth-

223

er." The man stumbled and slid down the wall; Peter rushed forward to catch him before he hit the ground.

"I'm supposed to save the world?" Peter said. "It's not even my world, according to you."

"Your world was built as a reflection of this one, and it was built inside of this one. It is your world. Save it, no. Read the history, read the writings, and bring the people back together. Rebuild and do better than we did." The man began to cough again, and Peter, now close, could hear the wheezing rumbling in the man's chest.

"What happened to you? You're dying."

"I am. I'm old, and I've spent too much time outside. But never mind that. Will you do this?"

"I don't know. I don't even know what is going on."

"Everything I've told you is true. Read, believe, follow the path set out for you."

"And what will happen to you?"

"I will die." Peter helped the man sit back on the floor, where he curled to the side and lay his head on the concrete.

"That's it?"

"Maybe. But I think it's likely there'll be more. Certainly, Johanna was sent by someone herself, just like you have been sent by him. I'm sure there's more after this. But even if there's not, it makes no difference. It's still this place, here, where the work is to be done." The man coughed abruptly, sounding as though his ribs were rattling against one another. A memory popped into Peter's head—an old woman spooning soup into his mouth. The memory breaks and two others sit across from him. Recognition overwhelms him.

"My family—" Peter looked deep into the man's eyes. "Will they come too? Will they come to this place?"

The man stared at the floor and thought for a moment before turning back to Peter. "That I do not know." He rubbed his chest with a decrepit hand and sighed gently. "I don't mean to be cold, but that isn't important right now. Right now, there is work that I have been doing all these years in preparation for what is to come. And now I pass the torch on to you, whether you want it or not. Please don't let it go out." The man coughed again until it settled into a low wheeze that rattled until all the air had gone out of him. With his eyes still open, the man was dead, leaving Peter alone again.

Rising away from the body of the man he did not know, Peter returned to the report in the other room, scrolling again to the beginning. He didn't know what to believe, what was real anymore in the wake of what the man had said. But he at least could read the history and make a decision then. If it was true, that he was in the simulation and had died, emerging into this world alive, then there would not be anything left to lose. In the meaninglessness of it all, he still had to act and to choose some path for himself. Somewhere deep down, though, he felt trust for the man and what he'd said. He didn't know why, having nothing with which to judge the man's sincerity or honesty, but to Peter, the words of that dying man had more weight than he'd expected. And so he began to read the words left to him. Through the words, he started to rebuild the world.

Lucy pulled the car out of the lot with Peter left behind locked doors in the sprawling residential nursing center. Nestled into the tree line with a small koi pond at the center, proofed against accidental falls, the nursing home looked more like promotional photos than the ones in their promotional materials. Sanna rode shotgun, and Ed in the back, as the car sped down the rural highway back toward Sanna's house—in which she would now be alone. No one spoke; all the sound present in the car originated from the car— the steady hum of the engine, the occasional thump of tires hitting rough patches of asphalt, the blowers filling the car with warm air from the heart of the vehicle. Even outside the car— with snow coating the ground and dampening the air, the songs of birds migrated away with their owners, the air still against the bare tree branches—the world was dormant, holding a breath, in suspense for what was to come, what the rest of Sanna's life would hold without her husband's normal presence. But Sanna was only projecting herself onto her surroundings; the snow had fallen from last night's storm, the air was still in the lull before the next one, and the birds migrated every year, leaving only stragglers to chew on the seed left out by eager birdwatchers. The landscape beside the road blended fully into a smear of brown and white from their speed, and Sanna turned back into the car, to her children, sitting silently with her, exhausted from the day and waiting to go home to their lives and find respite from the emotional turbulence of hers.

In the silence, it became clear how her care for Peter was only a way of escape for her. Through her daily routine of feeding and caring for her husband, she was merely refusing to recognize her husband's already present absence. *Would that absence continue when she was alone?* she thought. *Or would that absence slowly fade into the backdrop, no longer showing itself every day for what it was?* She looked behind her to her son, staring forward out the windshield, impassive but clearly grieving this sudden milestone to the passing of time. He caught her eye and smiled, reassuring her that she had made the right decision. She smiled back but did not need the reassurance—the decision had been made, and it was already too late to go back against it. Already, the tension of her obligation to care for her husband's health began to wane, briefly a repose, but soon the void was filled with guilt. She fought it with the weapons given to her by her children, but it would remain lurking beneath the surface; despite reassurance, she had still given her husband away, and it would no longer be her caring for him in sickness and health.

Beside her, Lucy had rebuilt her mask, no longer showing the breakages that had wracked her in the kitchen, no longer showing any vulnerability at all. But that would be okay. Sanna knew the fissures hadn't disappeared, but were currently being repaired in the safety of Lucy's inner sanctum, separated from the world by her emotional walls. She didn't begrudge Lucy of that. Instead she wondered of the content of Peter's experience for the last year as he slipped further into the seclusion of his fraying mind. *Was he aware of the descent? Could he even have been aware of his children's visit?* Sanna hoped that even one or two tenuous threads still connected him to the real world, that even if his world was primarily dark and empty, at least a few pricks of light were able to batter through the veil. Continuing down this line of thought, she wondered—if his mind was indeed blank and empty—if he were seeing the world as if in a dream, as if the sensory input was able to make its way to some ancient, cavernous part of him still guarded against the encroaching fog. Would these impulses project themselves against the walls of this cave, like a hallucinatory reverie, the symbolic content only understandable to the one submerged in it and its unconscious logic? He was neither blind nor deaf in his old age. So where would the sensory impulses go if there was no mind left to process and interpret them?

Sanna smiled to herself, finding the thought untenable. If there were sensory inputs, there would necessarily be processing and interpretation, even if only the most primitive. Even insects process information from their senses through their shred of conscious ability. Certainly Peter still had more mind left than an ant. By contrast, what if, in the absence of a coherent mind, Peter actually experienced the world more directly than her? What if her mind was a membrane that filtered the experience of living as it trickled through the pores? With modern theories of the mind, it was possible.

Her thoughts broke when the car braked at the stop sign marking the edge of the dirt road leading to her house. Lucy turned the car, and all three of them bounced inside as the wheels rolled over the rocks and ruts carved into dirt, now filled with a layer of snow and ice. They pulled up to the house, and Lucy put the car in park and killed the engine.

"Well," Ed said.

"Well," Sanna echoed. "Would you like to come inside for tea? I know you probably have to get back home, but just for a few minutes. I don't want to be alone just yet."

"Sure," Lucy said. "We can stay for a little while."

The three of them climbed out of the car, Ed waiting outside Sanna's door to hold her arm and keep her from slipping on the ice, and they made their way to the door. When Ed and Sanna were almost in the house, Lucy's phone rang behind them, and they turned to stare.

"I should take this," Lucy said, glancing at her phone. "I'll be in in a moment."

"Who is it?" Ed asked.

"It's nothing. I'll be in shortly. Pour me a cup of tea."

Ed nodded and helped Sanna the rest of the way in the house. Once they shed their coats on the rack beside the door, Sanna set a kettle on to boil while Ed took the teapot and several cups from the cabinet. As the kettle began to scream, the front door opened and closed, and Lucy entered the kitchen. Sanna took the water off the heat and looked to her daughter in the doorway, still holding her phone, mouth agape.

"What's up?" Ed asked. Lucy stood in silence for a moment, holding the increasingly worried gaze of her mother and brother.

"Th- that was the... nursing center," Lucy said. "Dad had a heart attack... shortly after we left."

"What? Is he okay?" Ed set the teapot and cups on the table and took a step toward his sister, as if to run back to the nursing center and resurrect his father himself. Sanna, kept motionless, her hand still on the handle of the kettle, freezing into a statue of herself, fragmenting and shattering internally.

"He died. They couldn't get his heart started again." Ed and Lucy sat across from each other at the table, collapsed into their chairs, and waited for Sanna to do the same. Slowly, as if afraid of the rest of herself shattering, she sat in the remaining chair, gripping the table, otherwise still completely frozen. Ed and Lucy grabbed each of her hands, as tears began to fall. Steam rose from the kettle behind them on the stove, fogging the window outside into the snow.

Acknowledgments

First, I would like to thank my wife, Kat, who read through many early drafts, kept me from getting bogged down in the details, and pushed me to consider and develop the characters more than I knew how. For supporting me in my writing ambitions in general and keeping me focused on what's important, I am forever grateful.

To Kim and Maude for your notes and encouragement on early drafts and general writing conversation—this book wouldn't have been ready for submission without your help.

To Jessica for being something of a mentor to me and always being available to give advice. My writing journey has been all the more confident for your presence in it.

To Cecilia for helping me get the book to the finish line, and for the entire team at Running Wild for taking a chance on it in the first place.

To Kyle for helping me learn how to sound like myself.

Running Wild Press publishes stories that cross genres with great stories and writing. RIZE publishes great genre stories written by people of color and by authors who identify with other marginalized groups. Our team consists of:

Lisa Diane Kastner, Founder and Executive Editor
Cody Sisco, Acquisitions Editor, RIZE
Benjamin White, Acquisition Editor, Running Wild
Peter A. Wright, Acquisition Editor, Running Wild
Resa Alboher, Editor
Angela Andrews, Editor
Sandra Bush, Editor
Ashley Crantas, Editor
Rebecca Dimyan, Editor
Abigail Efird, Editor
Aimee Hardy, Editor
Henry L. Herz, Editor
Cecilia Kennedy, Editor
Barbara Lockwood, Editor
Scott Schultz, Editor

Evangeline Estropia, Product Manager
Kimberly Ligutan, Product Manager
Lara Macaione, Marketing Director
Joelle Mitchell, Licensing and Strategy Lead
Pulp Art Studios, Cover Design
Standout Books, Interior Design
Polgarus Studios, Interior Design

Learn more about us and our stories at www.runningwildpublishing.com

About Running Wild Press

Loved these stories and want more? Follow us at www.runningwildpublishing.com, www.facebook.com/runningwildpress, on Twitter @lisadkastner @RunWildBooks